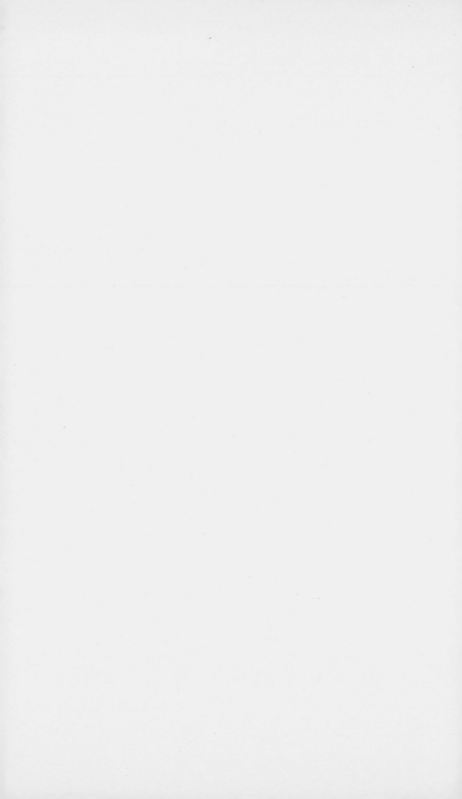

ITZIG AND THE HUNGRY HAMILTONS

"In life, the struggle never ends. When you suppress an urge, pandering to convention or ethics, it has its repercussion in the long run; it maims you or worse. Either way, you serve those forces."

William Hamilton

"Not even the dog will shit on your grave when you die."

Susanna Biro

AUTORITRATTO:
mire hoffmann

ITZIG
AND THE HUNGRY HAMILTONS

by
Imre Hofbauer

ARTHUR H. STOCKWELL LTD.
Elms Court   Ilfracombe
Devon

ERRATA

Page 108, line 45   *for* Anti-gone *read* Antigone
Page 112, line 25   *for* franc-tureur *read* franc-tireur

ISBN 0 7223 2451-0
Printed in Great Britain by
Arthur H. Stockwell Ltd.
Elms Court   Ilfracombe
Devon

Richard Church on the Work
of
Imre Hofbauer

Imre Hofbauer has made his home in England for many years, but his interests, and his reputation, are world-wide. The reason for that is found in his work. I see in it a universal compassion, naturally religious, deeply rooted in a love of his fellow creatures and the civic demonstration, architectural and monumental, by which mankind records itself as a civilization. I see in the faces of his portraits the same aspiration and agonies as appeared in the work of the masters during the Renaissance. He maintains that persistence of faith and dignity, in the time of stress and destruction. So his work is instantly recognisable as being lyrical with the music of the human spirit.

Richard Church.

Hofbauer's publications include amongst others:—

The other London. (Nicholson and Watson)
Bababukra. (Collins)
My little Englishman. (Nicholson and Watson)
The good time guide to London. (Houghton Mifflin, USA)
   (Riverside Press, UK)
George Grosz.
London. "Flower of Cities All" together with Richard Church.
   (Heinemann)
Monkey goes Home with Harold Kelly. (Collins)
Calvary together with Compton and Faith Mackenzie. (Bodley
   Head)

CONTENTS

BOOK I

Chapter One — Brydie and Hamie

On the evening they found each other Brydie sent her carriage away, after dinner at Frascati's, and they drifted in a haze.

The warm night fondled her bare shoulders. Now and again, she pressed her flushed face against Hamie's shoulder. In Chandos Place, the warm glow of the gaslight cast purple and blue shadows on walls and pavements. The bells of the nearby St. Martin's struck midnight.

As if from nowhere, a cab appeared. It ambled along, close to the curb, while the couple walked towards the Strand. Then it came to a halt, though they had made no sign to the driver. The warmth inside reeked of the slightly fusty scent of generations mingled with the smell of dry leather and timber, which permeated every chink of the vehicle.

As the cab passed the street-lights one could see, in the twisting oblong reflections of the windows, her small white hand laid on his strong one, while the suggestion of a smile appeared on the calm face with closed eyes tilted against his shoulder.

The driver, a stocky old man, had not yet received word from the couple. He let his horse strike a course for the river. As they stopped to gaze into the blue-black water and note that it turned deep silver in parts, like a fish showing its side, the old man confided that he had been a mudlark in his childhood.

The hoof-beats rang through the empty street and the stars as well as the lamps blinked drowsily when, at last, they pulled up in front of Brydie's house in Thurloe Square. The driver accepted a sovereign from Hamie only after Brydie had reminded him that mudlarks, too, must think of old age, which overtakes us all.

Her hand in his, Brydie led Hamie across the dark hall and up a wide staircase. He lifted her in his arms before crossing the threshold into the bedroom. So as not to break the all-embracing silence, rich with the scent of lavender and fresh linen, they whispered only the necessary words.

She undressed in the light of a guttering candle. In the last frantic efforts of the flame, her slim white body showed up against the gloom. His hand clasped round the slender waist, the man drew her onto his lap. Her head nestled against the white dress-shirt. He could not make out the few words veiled by her tears.

In the wide bed, even while asleep, he hardly relaxed his embrace. Her head in the hollow between his heart and shoulder could have been taken for *La Inconnue de la Seine*, in the gloomy light of dawn, if the warmth of life had not coloured the pale features.

It was mid-morning when, almost at the same time, they awoke. Stroking his face, she spoke, "Hamie darling, I feel that you have some fear of me."

A cloud seemed to pass over the man's face. He stayed silent. Then, as she pressed him with caresses and kisses, he smiled and spoke warily, "You know the proverbial danger of a little learning, Brydie. Here and there, I've gathered knowledge — it's part of my trade — and, well, I dread the horrid diseases. So far, I've been spared."

A shiver ran through her body and she paled. "I think I'm all right." Her words were steeped in conviction. "I can count on one hand the men I've had. I know you believe me."

In reply, he drew her to him.

They rested, suffused with memories of every moment since they had come together because of his ruse to gain admittance to her. It seemed to them an eternity, though in reality they had met hardly more than twelve hours ago.

With her lips upon his ear, she spoke, "But, after your caveman start when — metaphorically speaking — you seized me by the hair, you retreated into passivity, letting me do the rest. Your way with women! You have scores of them, I dare say." Without the bantering tone, she asked, "Do you fear them, too?" After a while, she added, "You've spoken little, because you don't want to lie to me. A man of your drive can only be a liar."

Hamilton put an arm round Brydie's neck and made a visible effort to speak, "I'm a liar, all right. I lie with ease and, to women, with gusto. But I was more afraid to counter your words — each one to the point — with possible flippancy.

"With few exceptions middle-aged women — widows and married ones — have meant the most to me for years now. They know a lot. Though I fight shy of saying so in their arms, they know the secret of life. Doesn't the phrase amuse you? It's worthy of a scribe in a women's journal."

Encouraged by her pressure, he went on, "The widow from Tokaj with acres of vineyard on the slopes. Her embrace was like the volcanic touch of her wine, and in her eyes lurked the wisdom of the soil, the same which mellowed the wine.

"The hard Hungarian winter was on the doorstep when the villain (Hamilton) pressed her to go with him to Vienna. Here at the Café Sacher the proprietress, smoking a large Havana, discussed with the aristocracy some of the more notable balls . . . .

"At this place Hamilton entertained the Curies from Paris, and Planck the physicist. The Curies danced the Mazurka like professionals. While Hamilton's imported gypsy band was chanting the song of St.

Peter on the way to Rome, on his shoulder his staff with a filled wineskin at its end, Planck smashed his wineglass into the mirror like a Hungarian yokel.

"He would repeat the party in her honour, the villain assured the widow. Through the smoke of his cigarette, he scanned her face. She may have known little of radium or of the quantum theory, but her instinct told her that Hamilton was lying. He did not want to take her to Vienna. However, she only said, 'Winter travel is dangerous. I might get a chill on the bladder.'

"For just a second, the villain seemed startled. Then he renewed the attack, stressing practical aspects of the excursion." Hamilton ceased his narration, to remark, "This is feeble." He kissed Brydie's nose, and felt the warmth surging up inside him. His concluding words sank to a hoarse whisper, "Find out for yourself, woman," as he folded her lithe body in his mighty arms.

Now that he had met this woman Brydie, he thought of the home he had never really had (his mother having died at his birth). He could see the manor Brydie, an only child, had left for the footlights with a smile, a pat on the jutting jowl of a hefty Victorian father and a shrug by way of reply to his threat to disinherit her.

He could hear the echoes of an Irish drawing-room and catch a faint smell of apple and moth-ball. He pictured the noble rivalry between maids and mistress over the ironing of linen before Christmas, the dry and matter-of-fact smell mingling with the fumes of glowing charcoal and the aroma of stew — Irish stew, a barbaric version of Irehély gulyás, thought Hamie — burnt in the heat of the tournament (yet to be served while the master's heavy eyebrows danced as snakes might to the flute of the Indian charmer).

Will she cook, he wondered. Can the woman of the British Isles acquire the art? Cooking is part of a culture even as poetry and painting are and, like these, it cannot be taught through the written word.

The dismal thought was swept aside by onrushing memories: His childhood amongst stable-boys and the children of the peasants . . . Nights in the study of his father, the inventor, by that time rarely at home . . .

As an infant, Hamie had picked up the modern languages from nurses and, before he had turned fifteen, he could speak Greek, Latin, Sanskrit and Hebrew — in spite of his preceptors; but they too had contributed to his education. One, an *émigré* Polish nobleman (as far back as Hamie's youth, and even earlier, Polish gentlemen had emigrated and lived on Hungarian estates "Like the king in France"), had taught him to drink wine without gulping. The other, a busker tired of the road, had taught him to roll a cigarette with one hand in his pocket and so on. The two instructors had found his genius a source of embarrassment and left him alone . . . .

Through his house passed a cross-section of humanity; it was more like a caravanserai than a home. This woman Brydie would make it a home without either new furniture or caging a canary.

It was not that he expected her advent would mean quiet and peace. Her slaty eyes spelt the becalmed Atlantic, but behind lurked the gale, the galleon cloud and the screams of the storm-birds. He had learnt that in life it was useless trying to weigh things up as fully as he did in mathematics.

So, he married Brydie Costigan, but not before scratching his head again and throwing a fearful look over his shoulder.

Three days after they had met the ceremony took place, on the way to Hungary, aboard the channel-boat steaming into Le Havre, with the skipper officiating.

Brydie's advent to Hamilton Manor brought no change, save for a cut in the personnel: Some handsome peasant women (whose duties about the house could not be defined) left, each of them richer by a thatched cottage and a few cows or acres of arable land. The Polish gentleman, the former preceptor and now secretary to Hamilton, arranged these matters.

The household had also inherited the busker, with whom Brydie struck up an instant friendship. "Kindred spirits," Hamilton termed it, as they could not talk to each other. The busker spoke only Hungarian, a language far from easy to learn. Yet Brydie mastered it in record time.

Chapter Two
Experts on Horses and on Women

A shiver ran up the back of the gently flowing Glossy, one pearly morning, as Steve stepped onto the bridge. The ripple upstream might have brought memories, had he cared to glance at the water. But he did not, nor did he look at the mill a little way upstream. He was oblivious of the song about himself, the mill, the miller's wife and the stream, which will be sung when nobody remembers him.

The song had not been born in the spinnery, but earlier. Songtree the gypsy woman had taken the new-born infant to the spinnery where, by changing a rhyme, they had washed the baby; then, by adding a verse, they had smoothed its tousled head. Only a poet could render the ballad into English, in all its fullness and Grecian economy of both word and image. Here is the story it tells:

The bumper crop was piling up at the mill. More, and still more, loads were arriving from the neighbouring villages by ox-cart and horse-drawn carriage, often driven by women. By the end of September, it looked like a regular bivouac. The mill worked late into the night.

The miller, with the home regiment, was in far away Bosnia. On the eve of his departure his wife, eyes full and lips aquiver, had sworn that the Glossy would flow uphill before she disgraced him.

She was short of hands, the king had claimed them all. The owners of the corn, old peasants and women, helped her with the work. So did Steve, just turned sixteen. He was almost the first with his crop; but the blue-eyed mistress of the mill kept putting off his grain, her golden tresses reaching her ankles as she combed them by candle-light behind the small window. When work was done, she would either say a friendly word or stroke his rosy cheek with her fingertips. And one night the boy's arms closed round her. His feverish breath scorched her face. In his iron grip, she lost her breath yet contrived to say in a voice as cool as the breeze before sunrise, "Don't, Steve. Don't, for our love's sake."

When his arms fell to his sides her playful fingers touched his mouth, then the down above it, before they reached for his hands. She spoke of her vow. She caressed the lifeless hands of the boy and buried her face in them, then she ran into the house.

Steve went on helping, but he altered visibly. His cheeks fell in and his

13

eyes assumed a feverish gleam. Though she no longer spoke to him at night, she once kissed his eyes.

Slowly, the camp thinned out. Only Steve's corn remained when the first rains of the autumn arrived. For days, it rained heavily. On the fourth day, there was an uneasy respite.

High within its banks, the gentle Glossy came nearly to a standstill under the gathering rain-clouds. The clouds piled higher and higher and, like a leaden threat to crush it, weighed heavily upon the surrounding puszta.

Thunder followed the sulphurous lightning and, simultaneously, the clouds burst. The floodgates of heaven opened wide and the torrents changed the gentle Glossy into a hell's cauldron boiling in cold fury, attacking its banks, lapping at the dike and rising almost to overflowing. A moment came when the river seemed to ponder, then, infinitely slowly, it turned — like the ebbing tide — and began to flow towards its source.

Rather revealing of Steve's shrewdness of mind was the episode evoked on his first hearing the words of the song which described the role played by him when the Glossy flowed backwards. He was not yet twenty and his first impulse was to bring his terrific fists into action. However, he thought better of it.

He considered seeking redress. He called on the lawyer, a gentleman of the old school with manners as endearing as a privy councillor's, who — "malgré lui", as he chose to express himself to the peasant lad — was shocked by the gross insult.

He turned the pages of a heavy tome — with such dignity might Hammurabi have received his code of laws from the Sun god — and embarked on a long dissertation on the nature of the charge, terming it "Defamation by innuendo". Twice he repeated the phrase, curling his tongue with gusto round the Latin words. "Pay down one hundred florins," he concluded, "and we'll see what can be done."

"How much can we make out of it?" asked Steve.

"Not how much," said the lawyer, "but your honour, my boy."

Steve left abruptly.

Afterwards, he turned a deaf ear when he heard the song. Clenching his fists, he would push them deep into his pockets — till he grew fond of the song and, when in the mood, ordered the gypsy primas to play it for him.

Steve, now on the threshold of middle age and with numerous offspring across seven counties, stepped off the bridge that pearly morning as a new gust of wind troubled the water. Chased upstream, the ripples hid the saillur which lay in wait against the water-grass, green against green. But the man did not glance at the Glossy.

His bearing suggested either royalty or the master craftsman. His far-away look only added to the illusion. Through unrelenting work, in addition to judicious land speculation, he had become a rich farmer.

Something seemed amiss that morning. On his lips lingered the stale taste of wine, and in his mind the even more stale thoughts on the arts of women . . . With a jolt, he was awakened from his reverie.

The Englishwoman rode her arab mare through the gate. She straddled her mount, which was almost unheard-of in those days. The dove-coloured jodhpurs, the ample gray cardigan, her pale face and light brown hair, with touches of old gold in it, made up a strange mimicry of the surrounding pearly grays, sandstone gateposts, dull green fence fading into gray above the yard-high sandstone base. A few stars and the yellow sickle of the moon yielded to the growing light. A lark appeared, a dot against the muted blue of the sky.

The picture resembled an old English print, accurate in detail and restrained — but for the mare which pranced and reared and tossed her head, to free herself of the pent-up feeling of the stable. The woman managed the mare gracefully, with her knees, reins in one hand while the other rested on her thigh.

Without a glance, she rode past the standing Steve. The latter appraised both horse and rider, as a horse-coper might, from under his bushy eyebrows. He did not lift his fur cap, did not even poke at it with a finger. His emotions were those of the impressed buyer but his face did not register them; one corner of his mouth sank in disdain and his lowered eyelids spoke of boredom. He did not end the ritual by turning his back on her — as she would not have seen it — but remained standing, his eyes glued on her back, till she vanished round the bend. 'She is different,' he thought. 'She may be, anyway.'

Slowly, he resumed his walk. He felt tiredness creeping over him, 'I'm getting older.' Only the day before yesterday, the barber had mentioned some gray hairs coming to light in the rich blue-black mane. He had dismissed the words with a gesture, but they stayed within him.

He had paid two calls last night, leaving the notary's widow at midnight and Jinie a short while ago. (Jinie's husband, having overworked the old custom of feeding the cattle on salt on the eve of market-day, was in jail.)

Steve had come away with a nausea. Jinie had haggled over payment. He was too much of a gentleman to argue with a woman and anyway, he pointed out, his price was fixed. She flew into a rage and spoke slightingly about his manhood. He felled her with a blow but his qualms took the edge off his punch.

While he was lifting her to lay her gently on the bed, she came to and put her arms round his neck. Her cheek against his, she sobbed. Her words came spasmodically, "Now you are like yourself in old times, Steve. You remember?"

He remained silent and she spoke again, "You took me the night before my wedding . . . . the night through . . . over and over again, for my own sake . . . ''

Still he did not respond.

Jinie paid up, but it left a bitter taste.

Steve was a prosperous farmer, yet his hunger for land was insatiable. The humble beginning of his near three thousand acres was the small plot of land bought with his first year's earnings as a horse-herd to Count Moritz Esterhazy's Hungarian horses.

He had been the youngest, and the most handsome perhaps, of a fine body of men chosen for their prowess as well as for other qualities. The Count took pride in artists finding them worthy models for their historic subjects when they painted or modelled the glorious past.

There was a dispute about the painting of Louis the Great who, to free the Christian maiden, had slain the Saracen. It was thought a great piece of art by prevailing standards. Even today one is struck by a certain freshness which the painstaking German school in which it was painted could not strangle.

The master herd sat for Louis and was greatly admired by the artist for his Asiatic traits; during the long sessions, he did not stir, never even moved an eyelid.

The artist did justice to Louis the Great. The noble features and far-away look spoke of a great monarch unconscious of the heroic deed he had just performed, the prototype of Hungarians, or as Hungarians like to see themselves.

When the picture was hung in the National Gallery, the storm broke. The artist — ignorant as artists are — was unaware that Louis was Neapolitan, an Anjou.

No one took notice till a reviewer, whose ancient Hungarian name could not disguise the even older name of Cohen, pointed out the discrepancy between Louis's arch-Hungarian features and his Neapolitan origin.

The clerical press entered the fray. They spoke about the reviewer's Semitic origin and advanced the thesis that, as a Jew, he could not judge on Christian matters. After a probing into the painter's genuine Hungarian name, the attack reached its peak in the accusation that the painter had been used, as a tool, by international Jewry to bring about the decline of Christendom.

While the battle raged ferociously in the columns of newspapers, journalists of all shades, clerics and Jews, amicably sipped their mocca in the cafés, discussed their articles (with galley proofs on hand) and opponents exchanged suggestions for increasing both the subtlety and strength of each other's writing.

Newspapermen left their cafés and swarmed down to the puszta, some twenty miles away (nevertheless known to them only from poetry). For days they grilled the unfortunate model. As a true plainsman, he stood up to this trial. The only statement they could elicit was that the King was an image of his grandfather hanged for highway robbery . . .

At last, the artist was interviewed. He agreed with both factions and spoke mainly about an indifferent world which neglected art. Then, in a more practical vein, he suggested that he could paint a new picture of Louis the Great freeing the Christian maiden in the light of his conception matured by the controversy — a highly edifying artistic experience — if the government, or a patron, would pay him from one thousand florins upwards.

Someone advanced the view that immortal artists were not unlike greyhounds; they ran best when hungry. Why not make another painting, anyway?

The painter now flew into a passion. His accents brought forth a twofold reaction. The liberal press grinned, the others lowered their eyelids — or cast their eyes to heaven — but even some of these had to admit a smile when the artist ended, somehow inconclusively, "It's no wonder that the country is going to the dogs!"

The painter's attitude was not exploited by either side, which made patriots speak of the high ethics of Hungarian journalism, and only cynics mumbled about the end of the canard season.

After Count Esterhazy's contribution, the controversy finally ebbed away. "In Japan," he said, "they paint Our Lord and the Holy Virgin with Mongolic features, yet we do not approach that art, or any aspect of it, with anything but reverence."

The horsemen of the Esterhazy estate had another function. Experts on horses, they soon became experts on women, too. Needless to say, many entered service with previously gathered knowledge on that subject.

The Count was a perfect host. In him were united the best traits of European and Oriental hospitality. He provided distraction for his men as well as for his women guests. So far as the men were concerned, the least scorned was when he brought down from Vienna all the women members of the Vienna Opera.

The women found it rather a nice idea to be initiated into the mysteries of Hungarian horsemanship by such splendid masters. Some even thought it might increase their social prestige.

The Prince of Wales, the Maharajah of Baroda and the Sultan of Selangor were equally at home at the Count's, guests who reminded one of the glorious pages of Debrett and *Almanach de Gotha* mingling with *cabotins* and other doubtfuls whose main income could be traced to the purse held by the agent of the Esterhazy estate.

At least in one respect, the years of thorough study bore their fruit. Gradually a new facet of truth disclosed itself to the horsemen and — through their agency — to the wide world, namely that the Englishwoman is the most ardent lover.

The heavy tips mounted and, after three years, Steve owned four hundred acres.

The horsemen were disbanded as, after years of activity, they were getting more and more out of hand. They literally terrorised three counties and they also fought battles amongst themselves. The death rate became considerably higher than the gendarmerie — indifferent as they might have been about the lives of peasants — could tolerate in the face of frequent inquiries by nosy journalists and busybodies and questions in both houses of Parliament.

Steve, by that time master herd, left with the other horsemen. The management of his land demanded more of his attention.

The trade through which he had founded his fortune became a mere sideline practised in his own circle, with less and less avidity as the years passed by, though he never ceased to be an idol of the women, young and old, whose salutes or homage he sometimes acknowledged with a nod.

The intelligence of his exploits reached legendary proportions, thus recalling an old belief according to which his end must surely be near.

Chapter Three
The Hamiltons

Steve came every morning, before sunrise, and every morning the Englishwoman rode by not seeing or just looking through him.

He felt for her as he had felt, as a boy, for the miller's wife. He almost rejoiced in emotions long forgotten and even managed to conjure up pangs of hopelessness. But he knew — and would have known, even if she had not given herself away by painstakingly ignoring him — that she saw his aura, as she saw many things. His instinct told him that she differed from other women. The thought persisted, against his earthbound reasoning.

When we want a woman we dress her in silks and velvet, he reflected. We may have a glimpse through our passion of the birthmark on her breast or perceive a jarring edge to her voice, only to forget at once and think her as good as a meal of freshly baked bread and grapes, as good as the mother we fret after and try to find in every painted skirt.

Then our senses tire, her voice becomes a screech, and her goodness only a snare in which we entangled ourselves. "She is cut as they all are," he rounded off, with the cynicism of the peasant. This, however, hardly served to stem a desire which threatened, like a spring flood about to inundate a bleak landscape.

Brydie was conscious of this force. She also knew of the legends which had sprung up around Steve.

She was the wife of old Hamilton, but still known by her maiden name; Brydie Costigan. They called her "the Englishwoman," as anybody who talks English — even an American — is called English in those parts, though she hailed from Connemara, Ireland.

At Collins Music Hall, Islington, London, Hamilton had seen and met her, a popular turn — the Rose of Bermondsey. The stage door johnnies had formed a phalanx apparently impossible to penetrate. So, Hamilton had employed a ruse which he had, later, termed a Hussar trick, and Brydie had dined with the strange "Irishman from Kurdistan or Zanzibar or the moon" — she had associated Hungary with distant parts — forgetting her patron whose coat of arms was a heraldic curiosity.

An emblem known since Norman days and gilded by vast riches, it united mailed fist and loincloth in a turquoise sea under a baronial crown. To draw Brydie into its orbit had been its last bearer's only wish. She could have helped him to spend his riches and forget the number of years he could call his own . . . .

Scratching his head, Hamilton had wondered what Brydie meant to him. Into his mind had come words read in his childhood, "A damsel fair with curling hair and such beauty as went out of Ireland when the foreigners came in . . . "

Five and twenty years earlier, he had met a woman in Dublin. She had shown him, above her embroidered garter, flesh as white as an icon. The pale Brydie had brought it all back to him, now in the noon of his manhood.

The student years at Dublin — always referred to as "my banishment to Tom's" — had followed his expulsion from Vienna University (the cumulative effect of paternity cases, duels and embarrassing the renowned Professor Horbiger, of "Welteislehre" fame, in his own field) or as the professor *collegium* had termed it, more courteously, *consilium abeundi*, advice to go . . . He had left with a heavy heart. By way of farewell he had stroked the worn plush covering of a chair at the foot of the huge mirror at the Café Mozart, where he had studied amongst crowds of fellow students, horse-copers, lively girls and business men of every description for whom the café had served as an office with regular business hours.

Once more, he had gone to Wiener Wald and sat down in a clearing. In the sun, inhaling the fragrance of the fern, he had been able to forget what humiliating experiences life could offer and Vienna's hardness on the Hamiltons.

To the glittering city of the 1840s his father had come, with brilliant head and strong right arm both for hire. He had brought grandiose schemes for lottery, racing etc. to enrich the exchequer, himself and, also, many hungry pockets. He had borrowed the means to lead a life akin to that of princes and barons owning land extensive enough to harbour the German principalities.

His schemes had not progressed as hoped and he would have been thrown into the debtors' prison, but for his invention, a new type of steamship. The creditors and half Vienna had thronged the banks of the Danube — while a band on deck had played a march — to watch "the inventor" board the boat. There was a shrill hoot, a puff of white steam shot into the soft autumn day and upstream went the charming little craft, new maybe to the Viennese, but not to those who knew shipping on the Clyde. The crowd cheered. After a mile the boat turned, then, at an increased speed, went downstream passing the onlookers once more. Fresh waves of enthusiasm swept the crowd, to abate as the boat grew smaller and smaller and vanished towards Hungary . . . .

With the help of her husband's secretary, Brydie fitted together the intriguing jigsaw picture of the Hamiltons. She heard of the inventor's misgivings about settling in Hungary (where the Rothschilds' refusal to lend money to build the railway had evoked the contemporary comment "It can't be good, if the Jew won't invest"). However, he had prospered and, on his death in the early nineties, had left a fortune to his only son.

In addition, Hamie had made a fortune for himself, as turf accountant, stockbroker and organiser of company mergers, thanks to what his professor at Vienna had called "the kink of the true mathematician".

He never lost the quirk for feverish activity. In the midst of stock exchange operations he heard the voice, and the solution to a mathematical problem found its way onto the back of a cheque, or a treatise on anthropology arose (usually first published in French, English or German scientific periodicals before being incorporated — in a revised, or more elaborate, form — into one of his books). His business and scientific activities seemed complementary, rather like the two coils of wire in an electrical transformer where the magnetic flux produced by the current in one threads through the other.

Every morning his secretary gave verbal reports on shares and on the chances of horses and jotted down instructions in a publishers' dummy — demy octavo, the standard shape of Hamilton's books (a string of them by the time he had brought Brydie home).

The secretary read daily scores of telegrams from all over Europe as well as the Budapest newspapers, and read aloud from the morning papers during Hamilton's twenty-minute doze after lunch. His delivery was an excellent soporific.

The Hamilton house appealed to Brydie. It was a place of great diversity, with unexpected ramifications, originally built by the inventor. A restless spirit, he had liked a change of surroundings. Instead of building a new house he had stuck a new wing, sometimes a single room or even a corridor, onto the already existing edifice. His son, inheriting some of his proclivities, also liked a change of scenery; but — while the old man had at times torn down parts and rebuilt in keeping with the original plan — the son, out of reverence for his father, would not touch a brick placed on the latter's order. He only added, and the result was a labyrinth.

One never knew whom one would meet in the long corridors, in forgotten chimney corners, in domed halls, in picture-galleries with works of Repin and Legantini, or in the indoor swimming-bath adjoining a dining-room, etc. One might meet the famous jockey, Cochran, dancing attendance on a handsome woman whom he had met on straying into a boudoir (the Italian Countess Z, he discovered later on). One met scholars, aristocrats, tramps, men one might pretend not to notice, two holy men — one from Pasadena, California, one visibly the holier of the two judging by his scruffier appearance.

The house sheltered anyone. You could come to lunches and dinners or — if you preferred solitude — take your meals in your own suite or room, or walk to the chain of pantries and, with your own hand, cut ham, apple strudel etc., washing the meal down with wine. You drew Heberrel from the barrel, or dug out the one-hundred-year-old bottle of Tokaj, black with time, from the web-covered corner of the cellar and drank the almost jellied contents.

There were children of various ages bearing the Hamilton name, adopted children. Nepotism without disguise.

Finally, there were the greyhounds, a pack of them backing up the guests dozing in huge armchairs. Guests and dogs seemed to out-yawn each other; they nearly swallowed their heads in their efforts. Who would ever know whether the guests had caught the contagious habit from the dogs or the other way round?

The dogs were the only drawback, in the house. They preferred to rest on doorsteps or thresholds and, often, an unwary guest plying between wine-cellar and pantries was forcefully torn from his reveries by a dog retaliating for having his paw trampled on.

The guests were rather critical of the dogs, but in vain were individual efforts to have them removed, nor was a deputation of guests more fortunate. On the question of dogs, Hamilton would not yield.

The older greyhounds became morose, often ferocious, as though frustrated after a lifetime of leisure, not unlike many of the older guests — generals and judges — who, when the opportunity arose, proved as hard as possible on their fellow guests.

Brydie fitted well into the coterie. She was in top form as hostess at the Harvest Festival of the money-lenders arranged on Count Esterhazy's behalf. The Count's income was enormous; yet monies were borrowed, perhaps to keep up a time-honoured custom dating back to the early days of feudalism — nay, to the times of unrecorded history. No true aristcrat would give up what became noble usage after his forbears had swooped down, from their eyries, on the merchants' caravans and borrowed from them. The sole difference was that the successors of those merchants did better, they extorted exorbitant interest, but they too ran the risk of losing their capital at times.

Hamilton once urged Count Moritz Esterhazy to abandon revering his forbears in such a costly way — only to provoke the wrath of the creditors, *"Noblesse oblige,"* they maintained, "and we, too, have got to live" and the Count went on borrowing.

On reflection, Hamilton himself found the custom justified. He remembered his father's words, "Ill befalls the people who fail to observe tradition handed down by their fathers." This exclamation had been prompted by a sudden drop in the consumption of plum brandy, throughout the country. The fact that the inventor had had a stake in distilling the spirit had not marred the manly sentiment.

Chapter Four
The Harvest Ball

The Harvest Festival of the money-lenders took place during the period of the harvest moon (the full moon following the autumn equinox) and commenced with a thanksgiving service in the church of the Franciscans. It was important, and this was stressed, that guests as well as creditors should attend the service. Such an attitude might have been thought somehow tiresome, as not all of the guests, and by no means all of the creditors adhered to the Roman persuasion.

Yet more important were the aspects of the ancient robber-baron/merchant relations. Nothing could be got from the Esterhazys by force. The land was entailed and the estate dealt with creditors in an autocratic way.

Once a year only after the crops had been sold, still standing — as befits the good farmer — was the Count prepared to deal, through Hamilton's goodly agency, with such trivialities as repaying loans.

Nevertheless the borrowing went on, and only Hamilton, acting as go-between, could beat the creditors' shrewdness. This brought forth the threat of a concerted effort to withhold loans, but they could not agree amongst themselves. Thus a great event, the money-lenders' strike — possibly unique in history — never took place.

The guests, often related to divers Royal houses, flocked from all over Europe and beyond, most of them by train; others, either domiciled nearer or against making concessions to a new age, came by carriage, with a hussar seated next to the liveried coachman. The men could not easily be distinguished from the denizens of Pall Mall clubland equipped by Savile Row, while the women could be seen, in open carriages, on the Champs Elysées as well as on the Nevesky Prospect.

As he would bow his head to no earthly power, Prince Radzivill arrived in a coach lofty enough to permit him to avoid bending his head.

These 'intruders' were resented by the perennial guests at Hamilton Manor. Some of the latter were crowded out of the armchairs where they normally spent most of the day (arms draped over arm-rests, lips parted and head tilted, they often seemed already deprived of life).

On the night of the Ball, the hundred windows of the manor were a sea of light. Not in vain did Hamilton hold, with the Japanese, that "the

23

source of noble emotions is the stomach — not the heart, as we in Europe make out''. A host of chefs from abroad, including a Chinese and a native of Goa, contributed to the atmosphere, enhanced by an international congress of wines and spirits.

The products of Marsala, the Rhone, the Rhine, Oporto and Tokaj, and the Widow, too, helped the Viennese band to create an aura — vibrant and almost tangible — of joy in the present. Strauss hovered over the hall, in the light of a thousand candles.

Brydie and the Count opened the Ball. They seemed to fly on the wings of the waltz, turning right then left. At arm's length, Brydie held up her turquoise skirt. She wore the Count's orchid above the brooch holding together the folds that left bare shoulders white as marble, with a blue sheen where they emerged from the tulle.

In contrast, a mazurka followed. The melancholy of its tune heightened the pervading spirit. Brydie danced in a maze of rainbow hues, happiness on her face, eyes glistening, moist lips parted and pearly teeth catching the light when she countered a partner's remark — a Fragonard drawing set in Hungary.

Often she could not even hear the words, and so replied more to the cadence, to half-suppressed words rich with emotion.

On the arm of a handsome youth, broad and tall, with poise suggestive of kings or Albanian goatherds, she said, ''The eyes of you Asiatics (thus she called Hungarians, ever since grasping that Hungary is neither Kurdistan nor bordering on Zanzibar) are most eloquent — like the talk of my people, blarney — but even more effective; speech without words.''

Then, again, dancing an English waltz, she leaned back propped on the arm of a Colonel of the Uhlans whose youthful face might have been cast in ancient Greece, but for the rugged black eyebrows and shock of silvery hair (One of his forbears sponsored the Golden Bulla, the Hungarian Magna Carta).

Holding up her skirt in her right hand, she spoke laughingly, '' . . . . your engaging lies, Colonel . . . By now, I'm immune. My husband does it scientifically, working them out almost with a slide-rule.''

Both Hamilton and the Count cherished awkward little episodes, such as seeing the scion of the old German family hold out two reluctant fingers when he deigns to meet the swarthy little financier from Bucarest whose economic advice he seeks.

Or the Dutch Countess who towers over her bandy-legged partner, his curly black hair setting off the pastel shades of her face. Life creeps into the pale blue eyes, then bloodless lips twist into a hybrid smile, when she learns that he is a collector of chateaux in France. In Provence alone he possesses four, with Daudet's mill thrown in.

At midnight, at the opposite end of the hall to the Viennese musicians, a band of gypsies struck up a lively Hungarian melody about the widow who stands at the gate remonstrantly calling her nine daughters; "Erssie, Pirie, Sara, Julie, Melanie, Ella, Bella, Caroline, Rosie, come to supper . . . "

The bands played alternately then, slowly, the Viennese gave way to the Tziganes, who conjured up on their instruments the wind sweeping down the endless Hungarian puszta. As the wind screams, there are hoof-beats of wild horses on the sun-dried plain. Stone is the bandit's pillow, the autumn shower washes his blanket. He is on the run, a thousand florins on his head. The innkeeper's lovely wife hides the bandit then, when tired of him, gives him away; here the wind subsides and a few plaintive bars of the first violin tells that the forest is mourning; the bandit is dead. The second fiddle and the cimbalom* take up the tune and, in a hoarse voice, the primas reflects, "Only last Sunday he drew the new wine."

A savage melody follows, czardas. It yet echoes the steppe of Asia. The tune stayed with the nomadic Magyars throughout their wanderings.

Brydie danced with a callow youth. With a few warm words she drew him out, in spite of his awkwardness, while keeping her feet out of reach of his devastating stamp.

After a few bars, she recognised the tune and looked round the hall in search of her husband. He, too, had heard the tune. He came in by the south entrance and she said to the youth, "Janos, I must dance this with my husband. Memories . . . You'll understand."

Dragging Janos by the hand, she landed in front of Hamilton, then turned and kissed the boy.

Hamilton — solemn, two vertical grooves between his eyebrows — put a finger under Brydie's chin and lifted her face. "Bitch," he said softly, yet loud enough for the youth to hear. The latter turned purple and, rigid in his misery, was at a loss. What should he do?

His problem was solved as Hamilton lifted Brydie off her feet and, as carefully as though carrying a Dresden figure, slid with her into the throng. Guided by prowess and instinct, their eyes interlocked and, thoughts banished by the consuming rhythm, they did not even glance at others.

The song from the vast expanse of Turan speaks of a people almost one with their swift horses. Like a storm, they bear down on a massive foe. After a short engagement they turn tail, running from the pursuers. The formations of the latter break up in the haste and tumult. Then the Magyars turn on them.

The woman in his arms hardly touches the floor. Hamilton alone goes through the movements, marking the beat by raising or lowering the slight turquoise-clad body. The instruments are muted, but for the few shrill bars of the clarinet that speak of the kill before the Magyar passion

* the gypsy piano

reaches its climax. In the ensuing whirl an exclamation echoes through the hall, "We'll never die". It rings true in the midst of the breathless rhythm. The dancers appear in a state of vibration like that in the air over chimney-pots on a hot summer day.

Brydie threw up her arms in exhilaration, then they came slowly down to her sides. Her eyes, which never left Hamilton's, seemed to gaze through a film.

Once more the Tziganes whipped up the tune which crept to a flagging note when Hamilton, pressing Brydie to his side, took her from the hall.

In the deserted vestibule, two hussars each holding a six-branched candelabra spoke quietly, unconcerned with the goings-on inside. They held up the candles when they recognised their master carrying Brydie. Half-way up the wide staircase, Hamilton stopped and said a few words to the nearer of the hussars. The man put the candelabra on the floor and hastened off.

Brydie now spoke, "I'm all right, dearie. Do take me into the trees."

Hamilton retraced his steps. Walking across the vestibule and out into the open, he beckoned to the other servant. This man, after a few words, also put down the candelabra and left. From the hall came the last strains of their tune, ending in three triumphant chords.

Almost in a dream, Hamilton stepped into the vehicle, never relaxing his hold on his wife. The old groom, who had quietly pulled up the horses, left at a gesture from his master.

In his warm voice, just above a whisper, Hamilton went on talking to Brydie. Snugly curled up on his lap, she might have been asleep but for the fact that her right hand slipped inside his dress-shirt and stroked his breast with fingertips.

On a winding path amongst tall trees, the cabriolet slid along sounding as if the hoof-beats were muffled. The rays of the moon came through the foliage, casting shivers of silver upon the path ahead.

With bated breath the trees, too, seemed to listen to his words about the warrior resting outside his tent and contemplating his wives brought back from his sorties — in olden times when the prayer arose, "From Magyar arrows, Lord, deliver us" — or received as tributes from vassals. ("The 'new world' terms it 'for protection'. It rings Irish," the imp in him stressed the aside.)

The blue-eyed Circassian woman tending the children, the gypsy who danced like a snake, and who seemed to dance even while carrying the heavy wineskin, the Cimber woman combing her long fair hair because the night was promised her, the Jewess . . . .

The dark Magyar woman from the upper Danube, with large sad eyes in oval face, the favourite before the Irish woman came. But the Irish woman was no booty. She came to rule.

They had cleared the trees and the horses came to an abrupt halt at the water's edge.

The lake bathed in light and, as a slight vapour, it gave up the heat of the day. The autumn tints of the trees on the far bank were reflected as diffuse pastel shades in the silver mirror.

She whispered his last words, "She came to rule," then added tardily, "until deposed." Their lips met in frantic attraction, as though they would devour each other.

His intimate gesture prompted her to undo her petticoat with a deft twist of the hand. She lay across the seat and, bending over, he covered her from head to feet with kisses, then buried his face in her bare lap. *"Das Ewig-Weibliche, Zieht uns hinan"* — the eternal in woman draws us on — flashed through her mind. Only the day before Hamilton had read her Goethe. Yet another image, "the kiss of Ovid," banished the last shred of thought, leaving her a sense of overwhelming happiness; he was all hers.

The same illusion held him captive. Words and images appeared in his mind as in a kaleidoscope; The hillock of Venus, *mons pubis, "remedia armorum,"* then — as if the *advocatus diaboli* had shaken the kaleidoscope — new characters appeared and seemed to linger beyond his passion; he saw himself on the journey through the Balkans, in his youth, going to the Turnu Severin whore-house. Here the woman with sunken eyes in oval face and full scarlet lips had spoken of the Turkish kiss — adding, while whipping the boy's senses to a frenzy, "You will do it of your own accord when you find the only woman."

They were part of the luminous stillness, Brydie's hand resting at her side — till it shifted, from the seat, to his head still nestling face downwards in her lap.

Not a leaf stirred. Slowly Hamilton rose, lifted Brydie from the seat, wrapped her in a blanket and laid her on the seat again. He alighted and led the horses round. They meandered, along the road, under the trees.

The hundred windows of the manor blazed into the night. The strains of a czardas embraced the returning master and mistress. Unobserved, they drove up the gravel drive. He carried her in his arms across the deserted vestibule, up the stairs and to the four-poster in her bedroom.

While he smoothed the eiderdown, she flung her arms round his neck. In her quiet husky voice, she spoke for the first time since they had come away from the lake, "You did it because you know I'm with child — your child." After a little pause, as she relaxed her embrace, she added, "Go back to the guests, dearie."

On the following day, processions from nearby villages converged on Tata. The population of the little town and surrounding villages assembled and came to the barbecue. The petty gentry — nobility of the seven plum trees — who had not been invited to the previous evening's ball at the manor came that night, so as not to miss the heavenly escallop and tournedos dispensed at the fire.

Deserving young men, undergraduates on the fringe of *jeunesse dorée,* received hints from wise fathers (who doubtless noted that there were numerous heiresses at the Harvest Festival, heiresses to fortunes from beer, oil and so on): Imitate the horse-herds and gypsy fiddlers who ran off with duchesses. After all, you can just as well supply their romantic requirements and, into the bargain, throw in escutcheons as good as those of the kings of France.

Chapter Five
"The troubadour in charcoal"

Much of the current Harvest Festival, since it was her first, was dedicated to Brydie. The Count and his agent vied with each other to amuse her with newer and newer attractions, such as the musical funeral of the gypsies.

The funds for this entertaining the lady contest, between the Count and the agent, came from the revenue of the former's estate (a matter of no importance established years earlier at the close of a court case. 'Earning' a great deal in the Count's service, the agent owned an estate which kept growing. He had houses in Budapest multiplying at a steady rate, a couple of steamboats on the Danube and so forth. When this was pointed out in court, the Count dismissed the statement with a wave of the hand and the words, "His father was good for my father, he is good enough for me").

No gypsy wanted to die and obligingly provide a corpse for the funeral. The Count, a globe-trotter, recalled a Texan claim that they had had to go over to New Mexico, shoot a man and bring back the corpse when they had laid out the churchyard round a newly-built church.

The pay for acting as the corpse was raised from one heifer to two fully-grown cows but, even so, no one volunteered. Many things happen in a coffin, trifling with God's ways or those of Satan, said the superstitious gypsies.

Some furious thinking on the agent's part brought forth a brainwave. He sent for Oscar Borichaner the major-domo and told him, brusquely, that Mrs Hamilton had thrown out a suggestion that he, Oscar, might act as the corpse. The agent added, confidentially, "Is there anyone who could refuse her wish? I would go through fire and water, to comply with her slightest desire."

The young man turned pale, a prey to conflicting emotions.

The son of a local Jewish cobbler, he had gone from the fourth form, at the school of the Piarist monks, into the Count's service. He began as an office boy but, by virtue of his qualities, his rise in the hierarchy of the estate was swift. He bungled whatever task was set him, but his willingness to amend and his honest face saved him from dismissal. Like a blundering politician, or soldier, he was kicked upwards — especially after his handsome face and proverbial honesty (a phenomenon in that setting) drew the attention of the Count.

He was barely eighteen when the Count offered him the post of major-domo. Before he could be installed, certain customs had to be complied with. There was a house rule, the single rule of the estate: Only a gentleman was eligible for the post of major-domo to Count Esterhazy.

On the Count's personal orders the carriage drawn by four white Lippizaners, with liveried coachman and footman on the box, conveyed Oscar Borichaner to the capital.

On the way to the Lyceum Roesner they called on the estate's tailor, who was to make a dozen suits for the new major-domo and who immediately fitted him out with one for the special occasion. It was easy to find morning coat and trousers for the slim young man.

At 4 p.m., after siesta, Oscar — diffident as always — called on the principal of the Lyceum.

The Lyceum Roesner, where the well-to-do sent their not-so-bright offspring, provided anyone with a school certificate — for a fee of one thousand florins — whether he had answered (or kept silent) when asked a few questions from the general curriculum.

The school certificate enabled him to serve for one year in the army, instead of the required three years, as a voluntary officer. Thus, when other means failed, one thousand florins were needed to qualify as a gentleman.

Oscar bowed on receiving the document with half a dozen impressive signatures showing the names of professors of the various subjects.

The ceremony over, our candidate lingered. His task was not yet finished. Really, he thought, the more difficult half was about to begin. He spoke in a voice which showed the tendency to falter at any moment. The coachman and the footman, too, were to acquire school certificates. He produced two one-thousand-florin notes, to stress his barely audible words.

The worldly face of the principal expressed astonishment, for a second only. He opined that to him a wish of the noble lord was a command. Less than a quarter of an hour saw both coachman's and footman's transformation into gentlemen by means of school certificates and the solemn handshakes of the principal.

Oscar's courage waxed. He waved four thousand-florin notes, stating that the Count also wished his Lippizaners to pass the exam. He wanted four Lippizaner gentlemen to draw his carriage.

The principal's mouth fell open, his close-set little eyes nearly popped out of their sockets, his hand rose towards the banknotes but stopped half-way. With a visible effort, he uttered the words, "For asses we provide school certificates, but not for horses."

Oscar, a fully-fledged gentleman, was still pondering on these words as the homeward-bound carriage transported him and the two other newly-fledged gentlemen deep into the Hungarian lowland. Perhaps, as they trotted briskly under the starry sky, the four magnificent white horses were not unduly disturbed by the fact that no change in their status had occurred.

Oscar was also an artist. Or, really, he was first and foremost an artist. He drew everything around him, in the ledger, on the backs of envelopes and of documents, whenever in the mood. His passion to draw claimed much of the attention he ought to have paid to the work entrusted to him and subsequently spoilt.

Oscar had a flair to draw character. The faces he drew on the accounts — of merchants who supplied the estate, the Count, the agent and gendarmes — had amused many, yet had hardly caused more stir in the sleepy little town than the birth of a two-headed calf or a good practical joke. They ascribed his fabulous honesty to his craze. He was a true artist.

Lately, he had made several drawings of Mrs Hamilton from memory (since he always drew from memory). She heard about them and sent word to Oscar inviting him to show her some. The diffident young man did not go, even when upbraided by the agent.

The latter took the drawings to the Hamiltons. Brydie was enchanted. She thought that the drawings divulged many aspects of her character, many more than either the mirror or the camera could. She wanted to buy them. Oscar would not sell but requested her, in a terse letter, to accept them as a present. She did. She also selected from amongst the Hamilton heirlooms a diamond-studded gold watch, a Swiss masterpiece of the seventeenth century. This and a daguerreotype of herself as the Rose of Bermondsey she sent to Oscar, begging him to accept them — "Though," she wrote, "the drawings are priceless and could hardly be assessed in mere money, they are more like me than myself."

The agent dubbed Oscar "The troubadour in charcoal."

Oscar, white as a sheet, only nodded his assent to act as the corpse when the agent conveyed the wish Brydie had supposedly uttered.

Brydie, in reality, was led to believe that she would attend a gypsy funeral, the funeral of a famous gypsy vajda — chieftain — in all its pomp as it drew past the grandstand on the way to the cemetery. This would be preliminary, at sunset, to the display of prowess by the csikós — Hungarian horsemen — in full dress.

To render the funeral proceedings realistic, the biggest house at Cigánysoron — the gypsy quarter — had been hired, a vigil was kept over the empty coffin and sorrow-stricken relatives kept on drinking the wine supplied (by the barrel) by the estate.

Over lunch at the Hamiltons', the Harvest Festival of the money-lenders was at its height. The hostess sat between the Count and the agent and the latter painted in words a vivid picture of the events to come. Brydie's interest grew till, suddenly, she said that she would like to see the "keening". Her words met with silence, an embarrassed silence, as the agent was not prepared for this turn. However he soon regained his wits under the mildly sarcastic smile of the Count, who even added to the mockery by holding his nose between thumb and forefinger (behind Brydie's back) for a second.

The agent rose, excusing himself. He had all of a sudden remembered a matter of the utmost importance which required his attention, he explained and begged the Count to take Brydie — when lunch was over — to Gypsy Lane, where he hoped to meet them.

Chapter Six
The Gypsy Funeral

The agent called for the fastest horse. To the danger of life and limb, he galloped over bridges, through streets and narrow lanes.

His sudden arrival caused despondence among the gypsies. The show was being cancelled, they thought. The wine would cease to flow. At once, the consumption of food and drink took on miraculous proportions. They drank as if paid to do it by the gallon. Whole hams and roast geese disappeared, swiftly vanishing under roomy skirts.

The agent's words relieved the gloom. He explained that he wanted someone to act as the corpse, "For a few minutes," while guests were present. He was willing to give one cow for the service. The gypsies remained silent and he increased the offer to two cows.

A middle-aged man spoke up. For an advance payment of ten florins — and the two cows — he would do the job. The agent eagerly agreed, which was a mistake.

The coffin was brought to the middle of the room, the flowers were arranged in a neat row, two tallow candles were lit at the foot of the coffin and the wailing old women arranged their skirts in seemly folds.

The man now began to utter doubts.

"What's the matter?" roared the agent.

He was tempting the 'Daemon Gazore', the man explained. It would involve him in considerable expenditure, to implore St. Sarah to intercede with the dreaded daemon on his behalf.

The agent found it impossible to argue on this ground. "How much?" he asked, his voice hoarse with anger.

With his right forefinger, the gypsy ticked off on his left fingers the items to be bought. Meanwhile, his black eyes scanned the agent's face.

"Two and a tanner for candles." He touched his thumb.

The agent's face showed no emotion at the price. The man grew bolder. "Two florins for incense." He tapped his forefinger.

The agent's face remained impassive.

"For a silver crucifix, to be kept at the bedside, about fifteen florins."

The agent, still unruffled, cut him short. "The total, my good man. Life is too short to haggle."

"Thirty florins," said the gypsy and the agent's calmness engendered

33

in him a new trend of thought. He proffered his palm. "Cash on the nail," he added, meaningly.

The agent turned purple at the curtness of the words and at being found out the moment the idea of default had begun to take shape in his mind. He fumbled in his pocket and brought out a wad of banknotes. There were only twenty, fifty and hundred-florin notes.

The man mused, "Forty florins in my pocket will be all right." He got the money as someone brought the tidings that the noble lord's carriage had just turned the corner.

The agent's threat to reintroduce the whipping-post was drowned in the strains of music and the feverish activity as the gypsy stepped into the coffin.

When the carriage stopped, a hush fell upon the house. Accompanied by the Count, Brydie entered on tiptoe.

At first she was hit by the dank smell of a house where the windows were never opened, where the floor — unboarded — consisted of levelled clay under straw and bear and sheepskin, and where the droppings of children and domestic animals were trodden into the ground. The heavy scent of the lilies was suffocating. The walls, hung with silk headscarves and faded textiles, seemed to exude not only the odour of generations living, giving birth and dying in one room, but also of those present who had been feasting throughout the night.

The Count and the lady stopped some distance from the coffin, where the agent barred their way.

The sob of an old woman broke the stillness. From outside, one could hear the tuning up of the fiddles. Then, as from afar, came the dirge played on the violin, "They laid out the dead body in the yard," which says, in words, that there is nobody to weep for the dead one, while the tune — mellowed since time immemorial — conjures up thoughts of the lowliness of man and the desolation of a past so sad that no rational statement can express it.

The susceptible Brydie was overcome. Her Florentine hat formed a halo round her head and in her wide-open eyes lurked something like the gaze of the somnambulist. The grandeur of the scene touched her innermost.

Through tears she looked at the dead gypsy, at the handsome swarthy face. He seemed almost alive. She dismissed the idea that they had used grease-paint. Surely, they would not paint the nose purplish, even if the chieftain had been given to earthly pleasures. "My eyes deceive me — the result of some strange refraction," she mused, but the apparent realism heightened the effect of the scene. She could bear it no longer. She fled.

As custom demanded, the children and grown-ups made a display of gratitude. They thanked her, in a chorus, for coming. They kissed her hands, the hem of her skirt and the earth she trod. She reached the carriage, with the Count and the agent on her heels, followed by many of the mourners who entreated the Lord to bestow eternal bliss on the noble lady.

She stood up in the carriage and emptied her purse into the throng, but hardly noticed the ensuing fracas. As though in a trance, she withdrew into herself and sank into a corner. The Count, on her left, gave the coachman the sign to start. Almost bewildered, he implored Brydie to come to.

The agent, seated opposite at her feet, bit his lip. In an undertone, he requested the Count not to reveal the truth.

The ride in the bright afternoon took them along the lake. A fresh breeze came from the water. A slight shudder ran through Brydie's body and the spell was broken. "Perhaps you aren't angry about all the fuss" — she turned to the Count — "but I was overwhelmed with memories. I may as well see the procession at sunset."

Brydie was not her old self when she took her seat in the front row of the grandstand. She met the remarks of her companions, the Count and the agent, with a nod or a faint smile. Other guests of the Harvest Festival contested every inch to get near her. Yet, in vain was the banter which, at other times, drew forth her sparkling wit.

Her solemnity induced them to reflect. By the time the funeral procession arrived at the railway crossing, their chatter had ceased. A slow train passed eastward, the travellers mildly interested in the procession at a standstill behind the gate.

When the gate rose, the procession moved forward slowly. Each group began to sing as it cleared the lines. The dust of the road rose to veil the procession, now gilded by the westering sun. A gentle breeze sprang up in the north, wafted the fragrance of the acacia's second bloom and became a balmy caress.

As the procession drew nearer, the singing gathered force. The voices of children and their elders blended to evoke a mirage of a distant land where vapour hangs heavy in the air, under a merciless sun which bleaches the skulls and bones of men and oxen felled by exhaustion; where a man in rags, harnessed to the primeval plough, stumbles forward — head low, feet sinking into the dank soil — while another man holds down the plough-tree with all his strength.

Only the tune the gypsies sing and the music of half a dozen bands can reveal the distant world brought with them, perhaps from the cradle of humanity, and enriched by motives adopted on their long trek from East to West. The Hungarian words do not reveal this world, though they allow glimpses of it.

The first group, the elite of the gypsy quarter, gathered round the banner borrowed from the primas Zsiga.

Under this banner, the heroic tziganes fought their battle against the oppressor at Nagyida. They fought for liberty and went down fighting.

The banner was rescued by a warrior who put it round his body, under his tunic, before the remnants of the defeated army scattered. In such a way, more than one banner was saved. In fact, Hungary abounded in those rescued banners. Judging by the number, the gypsies must have equipped as huge an army as that with which Napoleon invaded Russia; or else, every warrior carried a banner. The legend is vague on these questions and, strangely enough, no historical record remains of this battle supposed to have taken place at the close of the Hungarian War of Independence, AD 1849.

The men round the banner — the leading denizens of the gypsy quarter — wore either top hats or billycocks with their second-hand morning coats, dinner-jackets or frock-coats. Perhaps their parents, in lower groups of the social scale, followed behind garbed in the old-fashioned Magyar broadcloth, patches of red or green plush on shiny threadbare elbows, knees or seat allowing their passion for colour to creep in. Perhaps on the lowest rung the even poorer ones, in shirt-sleeves, brought up the rear of the procession.

Eight brawny gypsies put their shoulders to St. Michael's horse, the hearse. Dark faces above dazzling white shirts, black eyes deep under joining eyebrows, a sardonic twist to large lazy lips, sleek blue-black hair spoke of an old languid people who retained their identity because, shunned by other peoples, they were hardly better than pariahs.

Primas Zsiga's band was mounted on two peasant carts drawn by horses as skinny as if they had just stepped out of the biblical seven lean years. First and second violins and clarinet rode on one cart, cimbalom and double-bass on the other. This band gave the lead to the five bands on foot, which studded the procession at irregular intervals.

In rags or wearing only a shirt, and with fiddles too big for them, children of various ages — some hardly more than toddlers — circled the groups, their bare feet stirring up the dust.

Apart from the banner, the leading group carried in its midst a wooden crucifix from the castle chapel, which the agent had lent to the gypsies. The crucifix hailed from the Tyrolese village where, for hundreds of years, all the men had been wood-carvers. In their anthropomorphic endeavours, they had seen our Lord Jesus as a mountaineer whose clear-cut Alpine features express the concentration of one pondering how to escape a spring avalanche.

The crowd behind the band on the carts thronged round as if to protect, with their bodies, the young boys pushing a handcart with an image of exotic yet formal beauty whose pure lines suggested Etruscan origin. It was the goddess Babolna of the gypsies. There is no record of when, where and whence it came to the gypsies of Tata. The only reference to it, in the annals of the town, dates back to 1791 when Brother Lajos, the Franciscan monk, repeatedly upbraided the pagan gypsies for sheltering the graven image of a shameless hussy which would bring on them the wrath of Our Lord.

His prophecy came true. The good and pious people of the township took it upon themselves to act on behalf of God. They marched on the gypsy quarter, pillaged and laid waste, before the county hajduks and the Count's hussars could restore order.

Many of the gypsies fled. The unharmed ones — and others, after they had attended to their wounds — began to rebuild their homes. They did not cast aside their goddess. They swore that she had grown wings and flown away.

Sophie, the knacker's wife, corroborated the statement. She had seen witches on broomsticks descending on the smoking house of the gypsy primas Laczi Rac. Snakes had pushed their heads from the bosoms of the witches, had wound themselves round the statue and had thus formed a link between Babolna and their mistresses. Then the company had taken to the air, amidst frightening screeches and an overpowering smell of sulphur which had given Madame Sophie goose-flesh.

The evidence was generally accepted, as she was highly thought of as a holy woman. Our Lady communicated with her beloved people the Magyars, whose patron saint she is, through visiting Sophie one night almost every year.

However, the goddess Babolna must have felt homesick. She returned to Tata.

It was reported that one night each year, at the second full moon before the autumn equinox, there was a festival — a kind of saturnalia — in Babolna's honour. Her votaries, twelve virgin boys, received initiation. The gypsy maidens danced, their faces towards the moon. The moonlight bathed the lithe nudes, creating fickle shadows of luminous blue and violet. Legend had it that grief would come upon anyone who spied on them.

Last year Gabor, the swineherd, had found his way to the clearing where the gypsies worshipped. Ever since he had seen the maidens dance, he had walked with a stiff neck.

The gypsies were Christians but, as a people engaged in trade, they understood compromise. They retained their old gods and reverted to paganism in times of adversity — when the crops failed and when they were ill — or just because they were drawn to it.

With the volatile gypsies, Christianity was a thin veneer. The Christian heaven hardly stirred their imagination. In any case, the righteous would never allow outlaws like gypsies to enter. They would end up — how often they'd heard it from the pulpit! — in deepest hell. So they did not abandon the old deities, which were part of them. They were of nature itself which knows no sin, nor right nor wrong.

"It is one thing if ye lousy gypsies do something on your own and another when it's the wish of the Count, our noble lord," the agent had declared, both bribing them and calming their fears of the pulpit's reforming zeal. So, for the first time for over a century, they had brought the goddess into the open. Since no priest would take part in the proceedings, a wag from a neighbouring town had been invited to appear in priestly garb and perform the rites.

A sense of expectancy prevailed among the onlookers on the grandstand and below. The agent briefly explained, to Brydie, the significance of the goddess Babolna.

Then the accident happened, one that the stage management had not foreseen.

The homeward-bound cattle trotted briskly from the meadow. A few paces from the grandstand, the herd split. Some ran to the right and others to the left of the procession, except for the bull which would not move but planted his four feet firmly in the middle of the road. He was a magnificent white beast, of a stock from which the American longhorns stem. His lowered head spelt trouble. The effect was heightened by the word "gyilkos" — murderer — branded on his flank. They had branded him years ago when, as a yearling, he had gored a youngster. As he had grown, so had the branding.

Neither the crucifix nor the banner, the relic of gypsy heroism, inspired the first group to make a stand. Banner and crucifix thrown in the ditch, they scattered. So did the rest, as the bull charged.

The beast came to a halt in front of the coffin which the hearse bearers, panic-struck, dropped in the dust. The lid came off the coffin. Inside lay Oscar, his eyes closed. He seemed stunned. Then, jerkily, he sat up, mechanically touched the rim of the coffin and raised his right hand to his forehead. In his eyes, now opened wide, was a distant look. The bull stared at him, then, head down, backed a few paces to gather impetus for the charge.

As the bull ogled Oscar, the Count grabbed Brydie's furled parasol and, shouting at the top of his voice, jumped from his seat and over the grandstand rails.

The bull, like the cow in the famous Caran d'Ache drawing, turned only his eyes towards the distraction. The Count reached the spot and whacked the flank of the beast. The parasol broke.

The bull whirled round and gave chase. For no apparent reason, his emotions underwent a sudden change, the chase became half-hearted, allowing the Count to climb a tree.

The bull looked up, sniffed, realised that his opponent was out of reach and turned to trot after the herd.

The grandstand cheered. The gypsies came forth, from ditches and from behind trees. Leaving his sanctuary, the Count helped Oscar to his feet.

Brydie came to speak reassuring words to the young man, whose feverish eyes stood out from his face. He still seemed bemused. With hardly a word, he turned away and took the road for the town.

Chapter Seven
The Family Tree

The four-poster which harboured Brydie during her long confinement was, in a sense, a family relic of the Hamiltons. The inventor had had it sent from Dublin. For countless generations, Hamiltons might have been born, dreamed and died in it. In fact, one of the posts might have been carved from the wood of a mighty tree originally felled for the building of King Solomon's house.

Leah, one of the principal of King Solomon's seven hundred wives, gave birth to the man of genius who founded the family, answering — for the last thousand years or so — to the name of Hamilton, and whose characteristic, an irascible strain, asserted itself in each successive generation.

The family tree had been prepared by Signor del Imagine of Urbino, a genealogist of high repute who — for a further material consideration — would have traced the family history back to the far-sighted forefather who, urged on by an inventive mind, had left the primeval mud for firm ground.

The inventor, remembering the fee involved, had thanked the genealogist for his excellent work and success in reaching back to King Solomon, but asked him not to continue his research into the dim ages, as some of the evidence — inevitably slight at some juncture, in comparison with discoveries so far made — might have an adverse effect and even detract from the strength of the family oak. Slender roots might not be able to support the mighty trunk and branches.

"Would it not be a pity, my dear del Imagine," the inventor had concluded, "to cast a shadow on the existing structure where every joint is dovetailed with another?

"What good would come of going back aeons, to find that Atlantis was once part of Scotland and my forefather its emperor? I don't doubt your words, of course. I, like yourself possessing the artist's discernment, know that there are testimonies more compelling than mere facts. But, as an artist, I also have some qualms or — I had better call it by its name — superstition. I am reluctant to delve into the dim past, courting ill luck."

"You are wrong, my dear fellow," the inventor wrote, in answer to a letter from the genealogist, "nothing so practical as 'social ambitions' or as the English would say, snobbishness, prompted me to engage your services. Ancestor worship is an essential part of us. Amongst other legacies, I wanted to provide my new-born son with sufficient material to worship. Thanks to your art, we have succeeded beyond expectation."

One more letter from the inventor, in reply to a host of letters from the genealogist, closed the affair. "Dear Signor del Imagine, I note your enthusiasm to trace the family history prior to King Solomon. By all means, go ahead and do so in comfort. I take no advantage of your generous offer to reduce the original sum by half which, as you remark, would barely support you in your endeavours. I pray you, do not send on the result. But, why not write it up as a novel? Herewith, I give you permission to use the names of the Hamiltons, living or dead, you would like to include. Whatever you divulge, I promise you will come to no harm.

"For details about me, you may apply to my secretary who is keeping a black book of my doings for future reference — to wit, to blackmail me.

"You have overlooked a point in my previous letter; you again refer to the family tree as a prop for my social ambitions. If I had any, the existing over-life-size oak would do the job. It dwarfs the family tree of any of the ruling houses of Europe. By comparison, thanks to you, the Bourbons and the Habsburgs are mere parvenus."

One sunny winter morning Brydie, contrary to her habit, remained in the four-poster in which so many Hamiltons might have been born (but in which, until now, only her husband had come into the world, to benefit by the family tree). She was preparing to have her baby weeks before the time. Later in the day she said, to her mildly surprised husband and her confidant the busker, "No shenanigan," a wish which they interpreted liberally. Life in the Hamilton household went on as before, the happy blend between time-honoured customs and rules laid down by Brydie as the leitmotif.

She had suddenly lost interest in running the household and staying in bed marked her abrupt withdrawal. The old man brought her the books she wished and music. He also sang to her in a halting voice which cracked, then came to grief in the midst of a higher note.

He hummed and sang airs he had learned on his wanderings, as a busker, all over the dual monarchy. His songs had come from horseherds in the depths of the Hungarian puszta, or from a shepherdess in the Transylvanian Alps who for months on end sees no human being.

In the shade of a pine, her back against its trunk, in the noon solitude the shepherdess hears the music of the spheres surging yonder from the mountain-tops. From a myriad of harmonies, she remembers those nearest her mood and weaves them into a song. She passes it on to the tramp and the latter asks for it again and again. In him, too, the song touches depths and evokes yearnings. New helpings of cheese and milk follow.

The grass dies, the shepherdess dies and the song dies with her — though, at times, the song lives on . . . .

The pathetic old man's voice of the busker adds to the longing. The last few bars merge into the husky lament of Brydie's ''Greensleeves'', upon which the old man lowers his voice until his notes sound like the few timid knocks of a supplicant at the door. He does not understand the English words, and yet he understands. The discoloured, pink-rimmed old eyes speak of the shepherdess, of gypsy dancers and of innkeepers' wives who loved freely and lied.

On the following day the old busker brought Songtree, daughter of the Songtree who had made the song about the Glossy, the miller's wife and Steve when the latter was a sixteen-year-old.

She was a middle-aged woman whose hair, prematurely gray and streaked with yellow, set off poignant features: a beak nose over pursed sardonic lips which, even when silent, seemed to move with song, or gossip, cavernous eyes never at rest — eyes of a beast pursued and sensing danger everywhere. Yet, her features spoke of calm, too — the calm of one who knew adversity but had come to terms with it.

At the sight of her, Brydie felt restless. There appeared to her mind's eye dead Angus, who had come back from the grave because his wife had failed to retrace her steps from the churchyard to the kitchen where, for two days, his body had lain before the funeral. She could no longer recall the face of the nurse who had told her the legend but, again, she could feel the chill of that winter night as the wind had screamed in the chimneys of the ancestral home.

Her body never stirred on the pillows while, with slow grace, she extended her hand. The Songtree took it in two hands, bent and smothered it with kisses. Brydie had known, beforehand, that the woman's hands would feel like live eels.

Brydie's hand seemed as white as marble in the angular brown hands. The gypsy woman gazed intently into the small white hand before she released it and, settling herself on the carpet, arranged her many skirts into the shape of a volcano, from the crater of which her waist emerged. Brydie, propped up on huge pillows, looked at the strange creature whose eyes responded to the contemplative glance.

At last Brydie spoke. In her quaint, outlandish Hungarian she requested a song. The old busker pulled his chair near the gypsy and began to strum the cither on his knees.

''I thought up'' — the woman addressed herself to no one in particular — ''the 'Sheriff's Csardas'. I trust you will help me to round off the song. It's about the sheriff's fillies, but could be about the fillies of any man who takes a woman for granted.'' The silky tones of her voice dispelled the restlessness her appearance had evoked in Brydie. The few words uttered by way of a prologue were a piece of inspired showmanship backed by the strumming on the cither. At the woman's last word the old man shifted his finger up several octaves and produced a cat-like twang, a flourish of the cither virtuoso which earned him a dark look of reproach from the gypsy.

After a slight pause, her tones unchanged, she began to sing —
> "They say that the old sheriff's three bay fillies,
> Unshod, gallop the dusty highways since sunrise.
> Devil may care if they perish,
> Fillies with tread light as thistle-down.
> He can go on weeping, the old sheriff,
> I cannot help it."

As though the last line did not please her, she turned to the citherist, who seemed ready with his line "No one's to blame."

The gypsy shook her head. Then Brydie spoke hers, "Whoever can help it."

The gypsy woman repeated the words and softly hummed the lively csardas. The old busker followed her, floundering at times. Belated rays of a mirrored sun gilded the instrument on the old man's lap. Everything else receded, as in the Dutch master's painting. It was a cue for the man. Up came the tune from the cither unaided; a few bars, then he spoke the words and remembered Brydie's line "Whoever can help it".

Again, the gypsy sang —
> "Far away the old sheriff's gone,
> Looking for the fillies."

Then came treble lilts from the cither in the intermission to the next lines —
> "I went into his tiny garden
> To pluck red roses."

Again, she sang without words. Her eyes closed, oblivious of the surroundings, she made up another line —
> "The sheriff's wife was the loveliest . . . .
> blooming . . . . swaying . . . .
> autumn rose."

Bemused at the spectacle of creation, Brydie rose from her pillows. Her brown hair, the golden tones singing even in the shade, cascaded on her white shoulders as she sat up.
> "He can go on weeping,
> the old sheriff,"

came from the gypsy and, under her compelling eyes, Brydie rounded off the verse —
> "He only can help it."

Then followed the Songtree's modified counterpoint —
> "He only could help it."

The singing went on. Both the Songtree and the old busker shifted nearer the bed, as though drawn by Brydie. At a sign from the latter, the gypsy sat on the edge of the bed and her swift cat-like movement ended in again taking Brydie's hand in hers. Earlier, her cool touch had disturbed

Brydie; now it soothed her. The twilight of the winter evening gave way to darkness. The old man's suggestion that he light a lamp was dismissed with a wave of Brydie's hand. Quietly, he left the room.

Only outlines could be discerned in the timid fluorescence, from the snow, which the huge windows allowed to enter. A lively red spot — like a blinking eye — in the centre of the red glow from the white tiled fireplace strengthened the surrounding darkness.

"Ever since, he has wandered across the countryside," murmured the gypsy, just above a whisper, speaking of Oscar the major-domo. He had vanished — so Brydie had heard — after the ill-fated "funeral".

"He makes graven images, in dead wood or in stone, against the creed of his fathers. He foretells the weather and forecast the miscarriage of Potondy's cow. He has turned into a clairvoyant.

"The Brunner boy, the theologian back from college on holiday, was riding his father's piebald when he met Oscar half-way across the bridge on the Glossy. On his way to visit his lover, whom he had not seen for many months, the student's mind dwelt happily on the warm reception he would get from the blue-eyed wife of Count Esterhazy's master shepherd miles out of town, at the shepherd's cottage, while the husband and his lads were away at the Bicske market. So the woman's letter — written in a childish hand, each character resembling a sparrow's head — told her 'Beloved'.

"He recognised Oscar when the latter said, 'Don't go, Brunner boy. Courting her means . . . ' The rest of the words were drowned by hoof-beats on the wooden bridge.

"The student had to cross the Glossy once more. He covered the distance between the two bridges in a flat gallop, but his pace subsided into a walk before he stepped onto the second bridge. Again he met Oscar, who added, 'You're courting trouble, Brunner boy.'

"The student paid no heed to the words. Once more, as his mind drifted south to the woman, he gave his horse the reins. Only much later, on the hospital bed when his pain had gone, it occurred to him that — though he had covered the shortest distance between the bridges at full speed — the half-witted Oscar had reached the second bridge earlier, even seeming to wait for him. He was the first to voice the opinion that Oscar is the seer who knows the shape of things to come.

"The Brunner boy had been given a warm reception. Before the lovers could meet in an embrace, the husband and his lads had come on the scene. He had felled his wife with a blow and, helped by his men, had laid on the table and doctored the protesting young man. Then they threw him on a cart and took him to the hospital at nearby Tata.

"The doctors all marvelled at the skill of the operation performed, a skill no doubt acquired through castrating numerous sheep each season."

The Songtree installed herself in Hamilton Manor and with her came the lovely Ranoné, her daughter. The latter brought spring in midwinter, the aura vibrant about her.

Under her heavy knitted shawl she wore a pink satin blouse, her round arms bare and their hues like those of a peach cut in twain. The glitter of her large distant eyes — one blue, one golden — disclosed a wide range of emotions on the point of overflow. To full moist lips under a delicate aquiline nose, in an oval face, and thick brown hair (behind which she could lurk as though withdrawn behind a bush) her low forehead added something of a savage aspect.

Hamilton liked the singsongs. They stimulated him in his work. He sat in an armchair at one of the windows, face impassive, eyes distant, while the women sang the 'Song of the Highwayman', or lamented the sheriff's doings. He listened and, at intervals, pulled out his slide-rule, worked it, put down figures and mysterious symbols and made notes in a pad on the arm-rest.

Defying the doctor, Hamilton stayed on while a son was born to Brydie. His blue eyes, searching yet clear and without a trace of hardness, seemed to watch over the event.

The Count and his agent and other friends, kept away since the birth of the baby boy, got tidings now and then from Hamilton's casual remarks: "The boy gets lost amongst the horde of midwives," as he paraphrased the Hungarian proverb, or: "Signor del Imagine omitted Stentor from our ancestry," commentating on the new-born's vocal power.

Only a few attended the christening ceremony carried out by the guardian of the Franciscans, the beneficiary of a friendship he had struck up with Hamilton. The monastery received cart-loads of foodstuff to which, on rare occasions, Hamilton referred as "Bribery of the Christian Gods" (so he termed the Holy Trinity).

This attitude brought upon him the guardian's scorn and invective, both unlike the gentle monk. As the latter remembered the size of the donations the scorn subsided into reasonableness, only to flare again into white heat at another irreverence; once, for example, Hamilton chanted a snatch of doggerel dating back to his college days in Vienna, which alluded to the Holy Ghost's potentiality in love-making as merely platonic, *der Heilige Geist liebt ohne Schwanz.*

Hamilton spoke of his concern for the infant's salvation. Why shouldn't he be brought up to embrace other creeds as well, just in case . . . ? If this method were adopted, he told the monk, humanity would know no religious strife.

The priest scooped holy water from the font. His hand straightened and his forefinger left the mark of the cross on the babe's forehead. The latter was still moist when the little procession — headed by Brydie and flanked by Ranoné and the Songtree — was leaving the church. Doubts arose amongst the women as to whether they should wipe off the moisture before stepping into the cold.

Hamilton's deep voice stilled the qualms, "Of course, no harm could come of holy water."

Chapter Eight
The Carving in the Tree-trunk

The infant found two homes, his parents' bedroom and Ranoné's room
— on the same floor, though in the other wing of the mansion. Ranoné
was another mother to him, but for the milk which the infant in vain
demanded from her.

Brydie had decided to give her full attention to raising the child and,
just like a peasant woman, share the cares and chores with Ranoné.

"She is like a sister to me, the sister I never had," said Brydie to
herself. "The child loves her." She felt the tears welling up but could not
define her feelings. There now appeared to her the reed-bordered
landscape along which she had driven last autumn. Above it, the golden
vapour seemed to envelope her husband's face. "Hamie loves her, too."
She made a slight movement of the shoulder as though she could dismiss
the thought with a shrug.

A dozen cradles had been made by the carpenters and placed in various
rooms of the house, but discarded on the advice of the family doctor. In
the light of the latest discoveries, it appeared, cradle rocking affected the
brain. Books on baby care, in various languages, piled up in the
household. The Count's contribution, collected works of Pestalozzi and
Jean Jacques Rousseau's educational novel *Émile*, was found somehow
premature.

By now, Hamilton was often absent. His work took him away at
intervals, for more than a year. On each return the baby looked at him
with big blue eyes — the Hamilton legacy — as if seeing him for the first
time.

He would stay a few days, stand by while the women bathed,
powdered and dressed the child and listen to Brydie's or Ranoné's
accounts of the baby's exploits with a warm and attentive smile. Only
Brydie knew that he was far away. Out would come the slide-rule from
his waistcoat, in the middle of a discussion on nutrition. He would work
speedily on a problem overshadowing all his activities, then take up the
thread where he had left it and stress his point that carbohydrates should
outweigh proteins until the infant could stand up and "Ride the apostles'
horses".

As before, guests came from far and near and filled the house as well as the armchairs. They clustered around the two women. Brydie, her outlandish charm enhanced by motherhood, recalled more than ever the moody Atlantic in its slaty vastness as well as luminous majesty. On the other hand sloe-eyed Ranoné's lazy movements were those of the voluptuous East, as one knows from the tales told, and from the accounts of the famous Venetian traveller or as pictured by Delacroix.

Something was missing from the casual hospitality now that Brydie was wrapped up in her child.

The more she withdrew from the big world, the more apt was she to take in local tidings which trickled in through the gypsy girl and flowed in measured words, subtly, in the varying cadence of the story-teller. More easily than the printed word, each story bemused the hearer, cradled his mind and dulled his critical faculties.

As the last rays of the westering April sun lit up the eyes of Brydie's portrait, above the bed in Ranoné's room, the heavy oaken door flew open to admit the breathless Songtree.

"Well, ballad-monger, what now?" said Brydie in a half whisper, pressing the sleeping babe to her breast.

"The clairvoyant has made it again" — the woman pointed a gnarled forefinger at the picture of Brydie over Ranoné's bed — "then master Steve . . . . " The words faded into an incoherent and sibilant whisper.

"Out with it, ballad-monger, drop the stage whisper," suggested Brydie.

Gradually, it transpired that Oscar had carved an image in a hollow tree-trunk. The bas-relief showed a little girl chasing a butterfly across a rickety bridge spanning a chasm. Watching over the child was a presence, perhaps an angel though without wings, in whom one could discern Brydie's features.

Her cast of features reflected the placid humanity of medieval Italian art. German publishers produced gaudy prints and swamped the countryside with them. One can only guess that these prints had evoked the process which expressed itself in wood, or in paper, with sublime feeling, well governed exuberance and a technical skill which compared favourably with the best of contemporary art, though Oscar had had no formal training whatsoever. Or had he, prompted by his illusions about Brydie, simply drawn on his own resources?

"Every part of it lives," said the Songtree. "The seer worked on it, for days, along the deserted road to the hamlet St. Nicholas."

One or two people from the hamlet observed the artist working like one obsessed. A grudging nod was his sole answer to the queries as to whether he was working on a wayside shrine. On the following day, a host of people saw the relief taking shape. As the days went by, onlookers from outlying villages converged on the hollow tree, with the artist working inside oblivious of the world outside.

Then last Saturday, a procession from the town arrived in the early morning hours. The clairvoyant slept at the foot of the tree.

People, knowing only the tortured face, now saw that tension had given way to peace in the sleeper's boyish features. In contrast to the bright morning light, the bas-relief in the hollow tree was enveloped in twilight, but for the face of the guardian angel exposed — through some ingenious carving — to the sun. The result was breath-taking, a humanistic interpretation of heaven — just, good, infinite.

"Let's see it," Brydie said, greatly elated, and rose.

Slowly, the Songtree shook her head. "Others had come, including the village mayor and some of the gentry. In the general hubbub, the artist slunk away.

"Farmer Steve, too, came, took a good look at the tree, walked round it and left. In the morning after that day" — the Songtree paused, then gave the breathless news — "the tree has gone, sawn clean off the ground.

"It stands in the parlour of Steve's house overlooking the piazza. He sent word to Oscar to come for the hundred florins he decided to pay for the work.

"There was an outcry. The Village Council began proceedings against Steve. Thus, they hope to pay off old scores — at last — against the wealthy farmer who has yet to come out of a deal as the loser.

"He told me, a short while ago, that he would be greatly honoured if the English lady would come to see her image in his parlour." Now, for the first time the shifty, little, eyes of the gypsy met Brydie's searching look. "He may even present you with the image, my lady."

A slight nausea came upon Brydie, reminding her of the first time she saw the old woman. 'Old procuress' was on the tip of her tongue, but she said, "You want to sell me?"

The old woman's gaze never wavered while she spoke softly, "I'm playing for bigger stakes."

Chapter Nine
"But why the flight and drama? . . . "

In the smoking-room, after five o'clock, Hamilton discussed theology with the guardian of the Franciscans on the eve of another departure. As usual, the permanent guests of the house were strewn around, like corpses, in huge armchairs. Digestion their only care, they competed in out-yawning the greyhounds. These noble beasts, which multiplied prodigiously, seemed to laze everywhere.

In neighbouring armchairs sat the guardian and Hamilton. The latter spoke quietly, not stressing any point.

"Of course religion is necessary, but a better religion than one shaped by scholastic cheek which builds up both the bogus and histrionics, to sway the half-wit in catering for the herd, enriching itself in the process. God left the husk created by priestcraft and dwells in it only in name."

The Franciscan marshalled his arguments but, on the point of speaking, was foiled by a lithe being who came up behind Hamilton's armchair and put a hand on his shoulder.

As she stood there Ranoné, in her shapeliness, reminded one of an hourglass. She casually referred to her "intrusion" and drew from her bosom a picture-card of Vienna at night, the starlit midnight-blue sky complete with a silvery moon above the 'Ring'.

A small button at the front of the white crêpe de chine blouse was undone, partly revealing a maidenly breast which — not too small, yet firm — was of a radiant olive hue. The monk lowered his eyes.

Hamilton handed the card back to the girl, with the words "Read it".

Brydie had sent the card from Vienna, where her husband had left her and the child on his way to Budapest. He had broken his journey at the home town, to collect the mail piled up in his absence.

Ranoné's fingers dealt with the indiscreet button while she read: "Dear Hamie, I am having a jolly good time. The Viennese barons are almost too cultivated, most of them brilliant *causeurs* in half a dozen tongues. Vicky has appointed himself my knight and shadow and thinks — at the moment, anyway — that in my case his gallantry has no limits. Whatever that means, it sounds beautiful and Irish . . . . "

His nostrils distended with a deep breath, Hamilton sized up the reading girl through half-closed eyes. There was something in the smile lurking at the corners of her mouth that made him think of cherry

48

blossom. Suddenly he had a vision of a Turkish townlet, of the lofty walls and shuttered windows which screened the blooming girl Bejaze — the white rose.

Ranoné was waiting but, as he did not speak, she turned and walked away. Her slow steps betrayed her hope to be detained. For a split second, she stopped at the entrance, tilting her head slightly and turning it a few degrees. Hamilton had a glimpse of her profile, then she vanished.

He sat there almost stunned, as if he had never seen her before, not heeding the monk's arguments which carried the promise of interminable length. He stood up abruptly and said a few words about pressing work while shaking hands with the monk, who was left gaping.

His measured steps carried him to the main staircase, then he came to a halt. The hesitation took next to no time. He walked on along the winding corridor sparsely lit by daylight above and by a french window which offered an outlet. Oil-lamps hanging from the ceiling, or attached to the walls smoked eternally, hardly dispelling the dark. A sense of bygone ages permeated the corridor as well as some parts of the house. He took no notice of a footman, followed by a maidservant, whom he encountered.

He saw Ranoné as he had first seen her months ago appearing as spring in midwinter, her bare arms under the heavy knitted shawl, her husky alto voice during singsongs. He climbed the back stairs, seeing again the supple fingers do up the treacherous button, and also her profile as he had seen it blending with the panelled smoking-room, like a fugitive creature of the animal world merging into the surrounding landscape. A poor simile, he thought; nay, it was invitation disguised as escape.

He arrived at the door. Its hinges well oiled, the heavy oak door opened noiselessly. He stepped inside, leaving the door ajar behind him. Her back turned, Ranoné stood at the window. She could hear no sound yet she turned slowly, as though another presence — or the expectation of one — had awakened her.

She flew into his arms, all nerves and reflexes — the inanimate about her, even her garments, turning alive — and yielded.

A faint light entered from the corridor. Ranoné slipped from his arms, rose and closed the door.

Brydie came home two days later. No carriage awaited her, as she had sent no word of her coming.

Her retinue was left behind. This was a dream come true. Arrival at a low ebb at the sleepy provincial station enveloped in a dull light, two shadowy porters expecting no one beyond a commercial traveller who would perhaps supplement a meagre tip with a current joke.

The baby in her arms, she followed the gallant Vicky — Count Victor Wasmer. Dodging the steps, hardly more than a ladder, he jumped from carriage to platform.

The only fiacre on duty was reminiscent of the London cab — and of cabs anywhere — reeking of the care and gaiety of generations, the aura of mourning widows or of a 'booky' on the way to the station or of prosperous horse-copers on their way to the hostelry to celebrate a successful deal.

Never far from Brydie's thoughts — perhaps just beyond the source where words spring from — was the memory of the cab meandering along the Embankment, Hamie and herself inside and the old mudlark on the box.

She lowered the infant to her lap and turned to her escort. "Look, Vicky. All the euphemisms about my feelings towards you could not keep you from coming to Tata. The preamble to your stay — dissertation, Hamie would call it — is not for your benefit, as a kind woman would say, but for my comfort. Of course you are an attractive lad who would don both uniform and eyeglass and ride into battle, if called upon to drive the infidel from the Holy Land . . . Just like some of your forebears, you would smile on the conciergerie's cart and refrain from any display of emotion while the rabble pelted you with eggs and stones . . . You're one of the best of your stratum who can write poetry, a clean-limbed nobleman, a maiden's dream.

"And most attractive about you is your youthful idealism, almost living up to that of the hero of the ditty of Hamie's student days:

'The landlady has also a lieutenant
Who loves her during her period.
He closes his eyes
And dreams of a hero's death.'

Vicky, I'm simply perverted, that's all. Your charms won't bring upon me 'the dark shame of womanhood'.

"You say it drives you to madness. I may outrage your sense of good taste — but no bourgeois morality, as you seem to me a cut above the latter — when I say I'm prepared to go to bed with you.

"Hamie, you say? Yes, I belong to him with all the steadfastness of a healthy beast; I've had no other man since I first met him. He knows this as he knows everything. He would not worry unduly about my side-stepping, if it pleased me. He fears no ridicule. Of course, if a suitor made too much of a nuisance of himself he might take him by the scruff of the neck and throw him out, both registering and storing every emotion on the victim's face. It would appeal to the irascible in him and might contribute to solving one of his scientific problems, in some mysterious way."

The fiacre had stopped in front of the main entrance in the midst of Brydie's talk. She paid little attention to the coachman, who had opened the door while she was speaking. She finished and motioned to Vicky to get out first. He moved as though in a dream. She followed, pressing the sleeping child to her breast, and dropped a couple of gold coins into the coachman's palm.

They entered the hall, where a few servants had gathered. She entrusted Vicky to one, to be served hand and foot, sent for the busker and took to the stairs.

She put the babe into the cot in the bedroom, where every object waited in readiness to receive mother and child. The old man entered, gripped Brydie's right hand in both of his, but lost in the ensuing theatricals.

While bent low, the old busker tried to raise her hand to his lips, but Brydie's arm proved too strong for him.

"What's the matter, dad?" she asked, searching his face.

"Ranoné's gone."

"God! Why?"

As if Brydie had not spoken, he added — his shrunken little face devoid of expression — "It may be better so."

She looked at him for a while longer. The scrutiny ended, she said *sotto voce*, "I see."

After a few moments, she became elated. "Who cares whether better or not? Has she gone home?"

The old man nodded.

"Send for the carriage," she said quietly, "and stay with Willy."

In the gypsy quarter, the horses moved gropingly along the deserted, dark and bumpy road with its few lamps placed at odd intervals. Dogs howled their acknowledgment of the strange intruders which, on two occasions, rose to a frantic height; first when the footman knocked at a window and inquired as to the whereabouts of the Songtree's house, then again when they pulled up at the house.

The small window of the cottage, the only one which opened on the street, showed a light and its rhomboid reflexion cast on the road was broken into many shapes by the geraniums adorning the window.

Brydie walked through the broken gate and came face to face with Ranoné, who opened the door wide. They embraced.

Ranoné led Brydie by the hand, through the dark kitchen reeking of garlic and the soil, to the only room looking onto the street. A guttering tallow candle created a golden glow that faded, through paler orbs, to a bluish haze and dissolved into flickering light patches and shadows on the wall.

Two beds with their sides running along opposite walls, and pillows and eiderdowns piled almost to the low ceiling, left free most of the wall opposite the window. There — above a dresser on which the guttering candle stood — hung the clairvoyant's picture of Brydie.

Ranoné lit another candle on the dresser. In its iconlike rigidity, it corresponded with Brydie's mood as she sat upright on the sofa opposite the dresser and contemplated her image.

Ranoné sat down beside her and moved closer when Brydie put an arm around her waist.

"Have they told you?" the girl asked.

"I spoke only to dad and he thought it better not to."

"But, you know."

"I can guess. I'd be a half-wit if I didn't, after all the mystery. But, of course, I thought Hamie had seduced you ages ago."

"I seduced him the day before yesterday" Ranoné said, and then gave her version of the afternoon when she produced Brydie's card and her nerves "all went out for him. And it pleases me to own that I planned my move."

"But why the flight and drama? You're coming back."

"It might break up your marriage, Brydie."

"Fiddlesticks! I can more easily keep an eye on you two when we are all in one heap."

When they were in the carriage Ranoné, with the picture under her arm, continued to argue — even pointing out bygone events as part of her mother's scheming.

Chapter Ten
Vicky

That year St. Bartholomew's-tide — with white violets, cartloads of them — was *the* day of the Harvest Festival of the money-lenders (held at Hamilton Manor, as usual, on Count Esterhazy's behalf). The Count's agent, responsible for the organisation, found it all but impossible to cope with the work. In other words, he had forgotten to order his henchmen to handle the arrangements — till the guests began arriving. Then, it was almost too late.

The scent of the violets could not overpower the stink raised by the agent because his assistants had failed to remind him. He threatened to persuade the Count to introduce reforms, such as selling an employee.

Of course, there was the day when a rehearsal of the real thing was held and proved no disappointment — fortunately, as one could not go back on one's word, even when said casually. The festival *would* be held in the sign of white violets. The strawberry leaves were already faded around the edges, and the wholesome smell which this foliage gives off in dying, mingled with the scent of the violets imported from Parma for the Harvest Festival.

Vicky, settling down as one of the perennial guests at Hamilton Manor, lived through both the days of the festival and other rigours of existence at Tata. He appointed himself permanent escort to Brydie as well as Ranoné. They made up a triumvirate, riding out in the morning. He would have chosen a martyr's death, to be cut in twain and each half of him to accompany one of the women when they had separate destinations. At a dance or a game of tennis, Brydie and Ranoné would each have half of Vicky as partner or opponent. As this was not practicable, the women vied in selflessness, each ready to pass him to the other.

At times, his sorrow overbrimmed — no man ever bore such a load of love unrequited from two directions at once. It was enough to break a super-soul, as he depicted in his ode 'to his two Mimis'.

He drowned his sorrow in wine amongst the gypsies, on the shoulder of a bearded clarinetist or an accommodating beauty. The little town abounded in those always willing to offer solace.

Then, again, in a flagellant's mood he wrote savagely to his 'ossified Vestal Virgins'.

This state of affairs might have endured, but a letter came from the war office. Secured with five red seals, it was the order to Vicky to join his unit at Budweis on the last day of the Harvest Festival.

His calling-up paper inspired a poem of infinite sadness. "Gone are my days of Aranjuez," he began, the tears running down his cheeks and into the wineglass. His head sank onto the shoulder of the old gypsy, between whose gnarled fingers a few nostalgic sounds rose. Then he thought up the refrain and title. "The last minuet . . . "

Vicky's people had been worried about the highly emotional boy. Through their influence, they had wangled him a commission with an infantry regiment in which the officers were mere employees, men without private means — rather than dashing warriors, as in other regiments where the officers, on many nights, spent more than the monthly salary of officer employees.

Vicky was to be tucked away in a garrison in one of the remote provinces, to protect the busy Jew of Galitzia or the sober burgher of Bohemia. In the process of installation, some of the womenfolk might suffer but one could rely on a father or husband of the sober type, indigenous to that land, who lingered over a pint of Budweiser in the evening and adhered to Luther's dictum "twice a week" —

Jeder Woche zwier
Macht Jährlich hundert vier,
Schadet weder mir noch Ihr.

Considering love a mere soporific, he came to terms over the damage and accepted a few 'green-bellied' banknotes — double the sum if his ethics demanded more — coupled with an appeal to his patriotic sense that civilian sacrifice ranks equal with the sacrifice of the soldier for king and country.

As for Vicky, the calling-up brought him a sense of relief, though he would not have admitted it even to himself. There would be less drama and more bliss, in the garrison town Budweis, amongst the fair German Gretls and Czech Ludmillas who gave birth to babes with tracts of Lombardy, Croatia and the far flung steppes beyond the Urals.

Once more he, Vicky, would feel irresistible, though pale beer would fill the mugs — mugs bearing such legends as 'Life goes but thirst stays on' — in the tavern while a barrel-organ churned out a sweet Viennese waltz and the fellows argued in measured tones.

Of course, if that tavern stood in the puszta, they would play a czardas. Swarthy, black-eyed, tziganes would play to conjure up visions of a bygone world. The fellows would dispute less about *that girl* but, while landlord and gypsies hid behind the bar and in corners, there would soon remain only a solitary guest.

Vicky sighed and consoled himself with the idea that one cannot for ever live one's life at fever pitch. But, while it lasts . . . . .

"Why not marry him?" Brydie asked Ranoné, during the last phase of Vicky's stay. "Castle at Lake Constance, house in Vienna (where I could spend a season with you).''

Eyes closed, Ranoné turned her face towards the gentle autumn sun, as though to feel its caresses. It was more of a reflex move. In reality, she felt that her averted face and closed eyes could not give away her thoughts. She stayed silent.

After a pause, Brydie spoke again. ''You mean, you belong to Hamie.''

They were sitting on a bench, between two plane trees and under a twisting bough, in the huge English garden. By now, the sun had vanished behind the foliage.

Ranoné nodded, then came close to her friend and drew her to herself. ''When I write my book — as I shall — the dialogues between us two will be short and to the point, often interspersed with nods and long silences.

''It will be different from the diaries of the blue-stocking whose intelligent conversation pieces — running into chapters — chant the state of the inflated soul.

''I shall give a twist to our present talk. You began, 'Why not marry him?' and added the advantages I would derive from such a marriage. I shall omit the reference to the advantages but retain your question, which I shall answer instead of waiting for you to answer it. I shall say, 'I belong to your husband.' ''

''You will write a book when I have gone?''

They held each other cheek to cheek, like sisters in a genre picture of the nineties. Ranoné kissed Brydie, then asked in a low voice, ''You'd call it a Judas kiss?''

Whatever contrary interests they might have had, they had scraped only the surface of the warm sympathy of affection which drew them together.

''No,'' said Brydie. Shaking her head, she added laughingly, ''But, certainly, it will seem highly improbable to the reader that a gypsy woman and an Irish woman settled their differences in such a civilised fashion.''

Vicky came along the gravel path strewn with fallen leaves. Face solemn, steps slow, his bearing spoke of the tension which never left him but was now obviously at its climax.

Ranoné quoted from 'The Last Minuet' —

'' 'Lonely, I sailed for quieter shores . . . .
While the bay was still at a distance . . . . '

''But surely Vicky,'' she went on, ''you'll travel in the red plush covered Pullman via Vienna where you'll cross the Danube, apart from that, not an inch of water — not even a wash, so drunk you'll be. Surely, you stretch poetic licence.''

Vicky slightly clicked his heels. He kissed first Ranoné, who was nearer to him, then Brydie.

''Wrong sequence,'' said Ranoné. ''You ought to kiss Brydie first. You owe her as much filial piety.''

Vicky seemed not to hear the remark. Brusquely, he asked whether they would do him the honour of dining with him at the Café Esterhazy, where the gypsies would play the celebrated Frater Lorant's latest song.

"Should love to," said Brydie, "but Hamie comes back tonight and it would be odd to be out."

Vicky did not even ask Ranoné, one could not take out a young lady without a chaperon, amongst the crazy Magyars.

He bowed and left, a man with a load on his shoulders.

When he was out of sight, Brydie commented, "What a problem it is to grow up."

'I shall walk,' thought Vicky. 'It will give me time to marshal my thoughts.'

Under way, his bearing changed. He lost his woebegone look, and when he crossed the threshold of the café he was already the rake, from his slouch hat to his gait.

It was about five o'clock. The sleepy gypsies either tuned their instruments or lingered over a cup of black coffee but, at the sight of Vicky, they awoke and broke into an ovation. The jubilant tune they intoned mingled with their shouts of approval, to speak eloquently of Vicky's popularity.

He recognised the welcome with a friendly gesture of the hand. Yet his face showed the boredom of the grand seigneur, which hardly befitted the boyish features. To the hefty blond behind the bar (who at the sight of him stopped doling out sugar, slices of lemon or tots of brandy to the waiters) he said, *"Rien dans le monde ne peut conquérir mon ennui."*

Her large hazel eyes seemed to imbibe the words. In her own modest way she was a heroine, an unsung benefactress to a small town by virtue of channelling its love life. It was a function, almost an innate quality, of her profession to hold together marriages which, otherwise, would not have lasted to the grave, and help the faltering steps of youth on the path to manhood.

Permeated by a warm coffee-scented melancholy, the place was veiled in a bluish haze of tepid tobacco-smoke which hid, or at least made inconspicuous, the vaulting above but for the columns supporting it. Worn plush coverings of a nondescript green, dull brown chairs, streaked marble table-tops and a huge candelabra (which beckoned sadly its many reflections in the huge mirrors) heightened the gloom of the provincial café. It was an institution which, since Turkish times, had housed generations of semi-nomads without a home and others who — though they had homes — found the café their real home, with cronies and new faces and the handsome woman behind the cash desk.

On one of the occasional gala nights a cashier from a nearby town, after twenty years of blameless life, made a wrong step. For one night, he lived his dreams, as a baron or gallant highwayman — and mutely followed the gendarmes the next day. He had slept for twenty years in the domain of a houseproud wife. She could not bear the smell of his cigar and her knick-knacks, everything in its place to the fraction of an inch and without a particle of dust on it, smacked of tedium.

As Vicky surveyed the place, his eyes rested on Steve, a man he always found disturbing. He had heard about him from the Songtree . . . The blonde — to regain the young man's wandering attention — asserted, "He's only got to snap his fingers at a woman and she flies to him."

"Casanova," he rejoined, without turning to the girl, then his words petered out. The man had ceased to be Casanova, but women still fluttered round him. He now recalled meeting him in the early morning while riding out with Brydie and Ranoné. The heavy-lidded eyes searching Brydie, like those of cattle grazing on rich pasture, the man had jabbed his felt cap with a forefinger. Brydie, friendly to everybody, had not returned the salute (so different from the deferential ones with which others had greeted them) but her back — Vicky had ridden behind her — had distinctly expressed disturbing emotions. He was thus defining his recollections when the cashier spoke again.

"They say the Englishwoman and the Songtree went round to his house to buy the carving the clairvoyant made. When asked the price, he said, 'Money cannot buy it.'

"The woman — she is the devil, too, not only this one here — treated it as a joke. She said that was the only currency she could offer now; but, of course, later on . . . Who knows?

"Master Steve pointed at the wall and let her choose one of the four pictures he bought from the clairvoyant."

'The one in Ranoné's room,' Vicky thought (incorrectly, as the picture he knew was one of the drawings 'the troubadour in charcoal' had sent to Brydie). On an impulse, he went to Steve's table. "I want to buy the clairvoyant's work," he began, his voice atremble.

Steve looked at him, with a glint of amusement in his slow eyes. "I see" he said. "What's your offer?"

"One quarter of my possessions," the youth said and started to enumerate his land, forests, holdings etc.

"A fair offer. Shows you are a connoisseur and know that the clairvoyant will go a long way . . . "

"Agreed," Vicky broke into Steve's words. "Waiter, a bottle of Badassony '87" — in lower tones, he added, "To pledge it."

"Won't you sit down?"

Vicky shifted a chair close to Steve's and leaned heavily on his arm. "When can I fetch it?"

"Fetch what?" asked Steve.

"You just sold me the carving inside the tree-trunk, saying I'd made a fair offer."

"That's all I said and could say. Ever since, you've done the talking."

The waiter brought the wine. There was the music of a popping cork. He filled the glasses and replaced the bottle in the ice.

As the session went on, Vicky gained a picture.

Steve, of course, did not doubt Vicky's word but thought that, as the young man was still under age, he could not dispose of his possessions. Nor could a valid contract be made, in the circumstances. Steve would willingly come to a gentleman's agreement, but would have to keep the carving till Vicky came of age.

Then there were snags. Someone else already had an option. Who? That Steve would not disclose. And the council had sued Steve for cutting down the tree. That might turn into interminable proceedings and, in the end, whoever owned the carving might have to part with it.

The wine flowed relentlessly. Vicky, champion drinker of the duelling *Burschenschaft* or *Korps* Saxonia, wept while telling Steve his tragic story.

Around ten an unruffled Steve steadied Vicky from sliding to the floor then, gently lifting the boy face downwards, he shouldered him — as if he were a grain-filled sack — and left the café with an aside to the head waiter, "Chalk it up".

Amidst the gypsies' swelling farewell cadenza he walked, holding Vicky's calves while the boy's arms dangled beside the tops of his riding boots. The wine which flowed from Vicky's mouth spasmodically — a long ribbon, then drops, a shorter ribbon and, finally, a pool — traced their route to the door and beyond. Such was the method Steve used to rid a man of superfluous liquid.

Outside, an onlooker untied the horse. Steve mounted, with Vicky still across his shoulder, and they set out on the boy's homeward journey.

They rode up the drive to the entrance of Hamilton Manor. Master Steve, shifting Vicky to his other shoulder, dismounted and held his horse till servants appeared. To one, he entrusted his horse, with the request to rub down the hind part with which Vicky's mouth had come into contact. Then, he wanted to be shown to Vicky's bedroom, as he was unwilling to part with his charge. A hussar holding a six-branched candelabra led the way along the sparsely lit corridor. While the man turned back the covers on the bed, Steve stood astride with Vicky still on his shoulder.

As he slowly began to disrobe the boy, Brydie came in. She commented on the skill and gentleness he showed and met his gaze, above a slow smile, when he said he could think of a situation where he would enjoy the job more.

She ignored the words, but asked him to join her and her husband in the dining-room and to tell what had actually happened. "Pecze" — she indicated the hussar holding the candelabra — "will show you the way."

She left hurriedly, as if she did not want to attend the whole ceremony. To Steve, her departure seemed more of a flight. The latter left behind vestiges in the form of a trembling of the hussar's arm bearing the weight of the candelabra, and Steve's gaze following her long after she had vanished.

He followed the bent figure of the hussar, who held the candelabra high as he warned of a step where one might trip or said where they had to turn. Through wide-open doors, they entered the dining-hall. Two candles were placed on the table where Hamilton and his wife sat.

The place resembled a cavern where man hid treasure, as the flickering light picked out the silver and glass against the dark blue haze into which the walls receded.

When Hamilton had shaken hands with Steve, the two men sat down at opposite sides of the table. Brydie, presiding, poured brandy into the glasses — the fourth one for the busker. In one hand the latter held a club-like object about two feet long and, with the other, he turned a tiny handle. "A Turkish coffee grinder," Brydie answered Steve's inquiring glance. She was again her old self — lively, unrestrained. She spoke to Steve and almost in the same breath remarked to her husband that no pair could be more unlike in appearance than the two men. "Graying temples apart," she added, in bantering aside. "Yet there is a bond, a striking resemblance, under the surface. To say it with the poet, Wahlverwandschaft." She met Steve's blank eyes. As an afterthought, she explained, "The kinship of elements."

The busker poured out the coffee, not much more than a thimbleful of the rich fluid for each of them. The aroma seemed to enhance the conspiratorial mood of the cavern.

"Actually, we're plotting," said Brydie. "Hamie and I wanted to ask you to enact your grandfather in the epic of the Songtree. We would both be charmed."

Before Steve could answer, she pointed at the smiling Hamilton. "Of course, my husband's grin gives me away. He won't care one way or the other. Very well. I'd be enchanted if you accept."

"A request from you is a command," Steve said, quietly. His palm brushed his forehead, an instinctive move to conjure up memories. "As a boy, I used to recite patriotic poems on the Ides of March." He scrambled to his feet. Mellowed by wine and the loveliest woman he'd ever met — and with his critical and scheming faculties dormant — he thought it best to go now. Hereafter would come decline.

"You won't go yet, Master Steve," said Brydie. "What about Vicky? Talk freely. Hamie isn't with us; the polite grin is a mask behind which he's chewing the cud. During dinner, he had an argument with Professor Eötvös." The brandy remained standing and the coffee turned cold, in front of Hamilton.

"In the Estie" — Café Esterhazy — "the young man made me an offer," Steve began. "He wanted to sign away one quarter of his possessions for the carving of you. When I pointed out that he's not yet of age and therefore couldn't do so, he made another suggestion — a gentleman's agreement, he would pay when he comes of age. I told him that someone else already has an option. He was desolate. He wanted to take the tree-trunk to his quarters at the garrison town and worship at it as before the altar. If he had a woman to share his lonely life, they would both worship.

"Of course, I could follow the trend behind his youthful abandon. He did not think it out but there lives in him — way behind, in recesses one never cares to air — a sense of certainty that he won't need to pay for his follies when the clock strikes. Parental wisdom and the law of the country will see to that.

"Yet, I had a good mind to tell him the anecdote of the German princeling who, offering his hand, won the hearts of the loveliest in the land. He could never live up to his words, thanks to his sense of duty — greater than himself — towards king, country and, last of all, his family. If he got a woman in trouble, he sent her a prayer-book with gilt edges and bound in morocco.

"At last, I came round to the effort; but he was already too far gone."

Chapter Eleven
"Our bond won't dissolve . . . "

Steve stepped into the kitchen. To most people, he would have seemed as strong and deliberate as ever. Yet he did not deceive the trained eye of the Songtree. In spite of his calm and fatalistic dark eyes and his steady hand as he pointed at the door, there it was — plain enough for her to see — his end was near.

"The woman is very ill. Fetch the doctor at once." He made a slow half-turn towards the open kitchen door, then lingered as though he wanted to say more.

Slowly, his steps dragging, he walked out, into the sunny morning. The fallen leaves paved his way. A dull pain in his right shoulder, he rummaged in his pocket and brought forth a pipe and pouch. As he passed it from one hand to the other, the pipe dropped to the ground. He left it there. He hesitated, then turned towards the back of the Songtree's house. Walking through the garden, he hoped to reach his own home without meeting anybody.

He walked over stubbled fields, changing direction at the sight of a gleaner in the distance. His drag became more apparent. He needed all his will to walk on. More than once, he wanted to sink down — to rest in the sun — at the foot of a haystack.

For some time, the Songtree did not move. She sat in the ingle-nook, marshalling her thoughts. At arm's length from a beam, earthenware jugs hung from a shelf on which glazed earthenware plates, rich in colour, leaned against the whitewashed wall. Open spaces between beams drew the eye towards the twilight of the ceiling and odd shapes hanging from the beams; bacon, ham, sausages — the latter, many feet long, reminiscent of a ship's rigging.

Odours from the cured flesh-meat — decay arrested by salting and other means thought up by man — and the dying strawberry leaves suspended from the beams mingled with the scent from the hay under the oven, where the tom-cat slept, and with the dank breath of the mud walls. The whole — the warm smell of a kitchen dwelt in by people who gain a livelihood from the soil.

Particles of dust danced in the rays of the morning sun, as the distorted oblong which the window cast crept infinitely slowly towards the bed. At

61

intervals, a drop could be heard falling on the floor, to swell the pool of blood. For the most part, the pool hid under the bed; but a thin ribbon-like trickle flowed out, as if attracted by the oblong patch of light.

Only her head, propped high on the pillows, showed from under the eiderdown. The brilliant light hurt her tired eyes: she closed them after a few vain attempts to keep awake. And yet a part of her was more alive than ever, "It would be a good thing to behold my last morning. Before, an inflamed finger or even an imaginary malady caused anguish. Now one knows and cares little. No regrets — I'm going home."

The blood in which she was lying flowed from her and seeped through the mattress. She heard the drops, "There I go." She dipped her hand in the blood then, automatically, wiped her fingers on the sheet.

She was conscious of a chilly presence, of its breath. She opened her eyes. She saw dead Angus, of the tale of her childhood, who came back from the grave. His face blurred then fell into focus, changing in the process into the Songtree's face. By way of an answer, she closed her eyes to the gypsy woman's stare.

She was a child again, running beside the river studded with the masts of embayed ships. She slowed down, out of breath, on her way gazing at the sun as it neared the surface of the sea, on its decline, then slowly buried itself in it. It would rise again in the new world and beat down on the cabin of Uncle Tom, the old negro whom she loved and to whom she wanted to be a daughter.

The chill crept higher. It dwelt in her fingers and clung to her breast then, suddenly, relaxed its hold.

The oblong of light, now weirdly distorted, climbed the bed, up the wood, across eiderdown and sheet, and one of its corners reached the cheek of the woman who lay immobile — one would have thought dead, but for the slight rise and fall of the eiderdown.

"Die Sonne bringt es an der Tag — I can recite it without a hitch, but for the odd stanza when the tramp owns that for a few pennies he killed the old Jew who prophesied 'the sun brings the crime to light' . . . The Frenchman who wrote German poetry . . . The right poem for a mistress at a Swiss finishing school, for an Irish girl to choose . . . I fear floundering at that beastly line, though it's ages since I left Geneva — and Thurloe Square, too, where the sun caressed me . . . the mellow London sun — mellowed, Hamie says, by humidity and smoke . . .

"The Macassar lingers on my pillow where the dear old peacock laid his head. He left before I woke, to hide from me his corset and the crow's-feet, to guard some illusions about himself. Dear old soul! His thick white hair blooms in the sunlight — and so does his white moustache, with the tint of tobacco, over the pipe.

"In exchange for so much — house, carriage, bank account — all he wants is a little affection, a friendly word or a pat on the ruddy cheek. Or just pride in being seen with Brydie Costigan. He'll be desolate when he hears I've gone. As the colour drains from the face reddened by the sun of the Sudan, he'll say, 'I see' — the most he ever says.''

Once more she felt the presence, its clammy breath enough to chill the heart. Then it retreated before the onslaught of her thoughts. No. Steve's head had rested on the pillow. His image filled her nerves but, to guard her waning strength, she banished the image. Yet, it seeped in, converging on her mind from all directions. She gave up struggling against it.

''I have lain with him. He left to send for the doctor. He will never come back. He is ill, he won't last either.'' A tremor ran through her when a vision of him, in all his majesty, appeared to her. The clear-cut profile reminiscent of an eagle. The fire in the deep-set eyes tempered by stoicism and contempt for man and his values.

''His look softened when our eyes met. He said he felt once before what he feels for me; but the first time he, a mere boy, was wrong.

''Near him, I feel the elemental — the spark that moves masses — I am with the leader the masses throw up in times of need. The tame Christian name hides an identity akin to that of Batu Khan or Attila. A throw-back to the forebears I see in my dreams as the riders of the Apocalypse and the devastating Mongol horsemen . . . Genghis Khan, Timur of Samarkand — names that spell inexorable Asia.

''His touch evokes an elation one can hardly describe, his presence speaks of a timeless world where the Shaman reigns. Or am I merely an idolater explaining away the ghoulish appetite of my senses? I feel no regrets. I saw the Calmuck jugglers in the circus. Less remote kin of the Golden Horde than Steve, they did not recall for me the inscrutable steppe — as Steve has . . .

''It was hectic, but for a while only, and never like the bond with Hamie which — if the word means anything — is eternal.

''The hoof-beats. That's Hamie, he took the gate in a leap.'' A faint hue rose in Brydie's cheeks.

Quietly, a steady hand opened the door. Hamilton stood there. In a flash, his eyes took in the room. He walked to the bed and knelt down. Brydie's face with the hint of red in the cheeks suggested a sleeping child.

Squandering the last shreds of her strength, she turned her face towards the sun. Her right hand and arm lay above the eiderdown. He covered them with kisses. The heavy hand inside her, which had at times eased its grip, now relaxed fully. The well-being of the convalescent swept over her, she felt restored and thirsting for sleep.

The man rose, then sat down at the foot of the bed. His hands slipped under the eiderdown and caressed her icy feet.

From outside words were heard, then the trot of a horse. The doctor had arrived. There was a knock and, without waiting, a squat little man entered. He muttered a greeting and put down the little case, which was marked NOSTRUM in gold, on a chair at the door.

Dr Breuer's broad Semitic features spoke of warmth and introspection. He was completely wrapped up in medicine and in his patients, the great majority of whom he treated free of charge.

He felt her pulse, brushed her forehead with fingertips and, with thumb and forefinger, opened an eye. The deft movements — of second nature through decades of practice — were more than mere preliminaries for diagnosis. They comforted the sick.

"Did I say no regret, not even for Willy?"

As the doctor's healing hand drew away, the miasmal sensation returned — but for a second only — the pressure of Hamie's hand on her feet, evoked by instinct, drove it back into darkness. Perhaps the pressure meant something else, too. He was bracing himself to hear what he had known all along.

The doctor walked to the centre of the room, stopped there and turned his head towards Hamilton, whose eyes followed, and could read his lips. *"Est moribunda."* Then, in an audible voice, he added: "Would you like me to give your wife an injection?"

Not waiting for a reply, he picked up his case and left.

"No regrets, I thought. Yet, I'll formulate my thoughts. If I plead . . . . ''

"No, Brydie." Hamilton spoke in a low key, "Talk of free will is nonsense, we're puppets. Our actions are governed by cosmic influences, in the mass as well as individual action, to keep a balance — the Magyar proverb sums it up; the trees can't grow to the sky — or to act like a proper police force which does not aim to stamp out crime but to keep it at a reasonably low level. The individual struggles to defeat the influences, in other words, his urges and desires are but other heads of the dragon. In the myth, the hero wins by cutting off the heads of the dragon, one by one. Here the myth ends.

"In life, the struggle never ends. When you suppress an urge, pandering to convention or ethics, it has its repercussion in the long run; it maims you or worse. Either way, you serve those forces."

Brydie smiled faintly. He paused as she opened her eyes and, without difficulty, he made out her thoughts: "You're whitewashing me. It's doing me good."

"No. You know I dread rhetorics. I couldn't tell you this before. We are one and the same, a monster consisting of a man and a woman. We live the same life (the same emotions). I'm jockeying myself into an Irish bull, to make myself clear. A bull which is really a pregnant cow — pregnant with meaning. I said we are one and the same; actually, we became one because the bond between us is so strong. We follow the same urges, instinctively, but you never defined them; I mostly did — it's my trade. Thus, we often act in a manner which on the surface, in the eyes of the world, seems contrary to the interests of each other, but which in reality is just the opposite.

"You kicked over the traces as any spirited married woman would, or married man for that matter, and so there was no danger that through an unfulfilled desire you might turn into a self-righteous virago who rules with a steel rod in her righteousness.

"Our bond won't dissolve, not even on our parting."

The words lent her a new lease of life — or was it the sun, now almost at a standstill?

"Oscar will paint me. I may yet live in the sun."

Oscar's face appeared, his face pressed against the window. She spoke again, "Let him come, the flahorly one."

Hamilton motioned with his head. After a while, Oscar came, haggard and diffident. As he hesitated at the threshold, Hamilton said, "Come in. She wants you."

E

Chapter Twelve
In the Churchyard

It was All Saints' Day, the first after Brydie's death. Above the western horizon, the sun left a pale yellow ribbon which lingered above the dark flattened landscape; distance faded, as in a picture scanned for its colour with an eye shut.

Ranoné entered the churchyard, with little Willy in her arms. She pressed the child to her bosom. Hamilton trailed after them.

In the east, over the tree-tops, the blue hills — the last upsurge of the Carpathians before they subsided into the untamed expanse of the Hungarian puszta — seemed almost translucent in the depthless panorama under the autumn clouds. A solitary star shone above the clearing. The gate opened into the wide passage between brick walls built around Roman tombstones. One of these bore the relief of husband and wife holding hands. "A memento more articulate than the rocks into which the gods turned the Athenian couple," reflected Hamilton. "These, too, might have been devout when the battle which rages in us all ceased. While the senses are wide awake, we clash and make it up, the battle is followed by truce, only to break out again with renewed fury. If the communion does not run aground, if the boat holds at the seams, we might sail into veneration, the doldrums of old age . . .

"We, too, were destined to tread the path of Philomen and Baucis. If only Brydie had lived!"

As though she sensed his thoughts, Ranoné spoke, "Don't fret, Hamie. You aren't so old yet."

It seemed to him that the words were coming from a distance. Their meaning escaped him. Black-clad townfolk and villagers who passed them at every step registered as shadows the fluttering candles cast on the rim of his awareness.

They stopped at the grave. The small marble headstone bore, in quiet Roman characters, the inscription —

MRS WILLIAM HAMILTON
born Brydie Costigan
lived 27 years

Hamilton, with bare head and the mien of one far away, took the child. Then he stood motionless, but for his moving lips. He murmured a prayer, floundering on a forgotten word.

Slowly, Ranoné bent down and lit the candles, not oblivious that the move arrested the man's attention and communicated to him some of the languor and longing which came upon her in his company.

She struck a match. The line of her straight back against the white marble etched itself on Hamilton's mind, to the exclusion of every other thought, and stayed there for a while. Then his thoughts began to flow backward in waves fraught with association, which corroded the contour and moulded the mass into successive images.

Back came the indefinable, felt as a young boy when he followed his playmate Susanna after she had shown him the ring, her little fingers trembling with excitement. The infinite melancholy of the autumn evening seemed to touch an exposed nerve, it cut him in the breast. As the sensation travelled, all functions came to a halt and they both stood watching the brightly lit train pass in the night of inexorable and shapeless hopes. Years later, he defined the sensation as 'the sap rising'.

Now, he felt again the sultry air of Collins swept by a gust of the cool Atlantic breeze: Brydie's entrance, when he first saw her on the stage. The footlights fluttered.

On that memorable night, he overheard the remark "She is lovely, in a washed-out way, isn't she?" Again and again, he remembered the words. They, too, spelt the slaty Atlantic. He could also feel again the cool caress on his forehead, then the soothing palm, as the hansom cab ambled along.

In the churchyard which — with its will-o'-the-wisp lights — had receded behind the images of the past, Hamilton reflected, 'Every creation is rooted in ferment and strife. I accepted the scholarly view handed down through the ages. The lack of struggle in our relations denies the view and opens a new vista.

'She gave herself fully. She revolved in me and fused with me. I derived immense strength from it. But was strife really fully absent? Did I paint a picture of make-believe? The same I am grafting on relations between myself and Ranoné? I am taking her for granted. My imagining that Brydie handed the club to Ranoné, as in a relay race, is faulty. Inevitable, with analogies designed to lull my qualms.'

They left Brydie's grave. The flowers sheltered the flickering candles.

Hamilton, with Willy in his arms, led the way. The long strides stressed his quixotic aspect amongst tombstones sparsely lit against the volatile reflections of lights on the lilac leaves.

Ranoné caught up with them, at a grave with a small marble slab sunk into its side —

Susanna Biro, maiden,
lived 14 years

Ranoné's ready smile met his peasant ribaldry: "Not even the dog will shit on your grave when you die." In his slow reflective way he added that those were the words Susanna said when, as children, they played in the churchyard. "Laugh, by all means," he encouraged Ranoné as, a spark of mischief in her eyes, she struggled hard to suppress her mirth.

She spoke, at last. "Do tell, Hamie. Don't keep it all to yourself."

"For a few years, I almost lost sight of her. She was there, of course. She lived with her parents in the old village. I remember a red ribbon in her hair, her eyes cast low when we met in the street.

"Then, one day, I met her in front of the Swan Tavern. Excitedly, she showed me the ring round her middle finger, a thin golden wire twisted in its course into an R. I teased her, saying that R did not stand for Susanna.

"The idea cast a shadow on her joy but she assured me that R was next door to S. On our way, bantering, we passed the churchyard. At the north side, along the railway lines, she shifted a wooden pale in the fence and climbed in. That was her secret entrance, as she often played there.

"I might have left her but when she turned her head to me, in the opening, I felt the sensation for the first time in all its freshness. All my senses awoke. That year, the acacia bloomed a second time. The scent enveloped me, caressed me. I felt an urge to run but, at the same time, I knew I would follow her. We ambled amongst the graves, the nostalgia in me expanded. There was not a bird in the air, not a leaf stirred under the light of the setting sun. Life had come to a standstill.

"She pulled the ring from her finger, played with it, then feigned throwing it to me. She repeated this. The third time, when she let it go, I took no notice. It fell into the thick undergrowth. We looked for it, on our knees, but could not find it. We found happiness, instead.

"We met every day till my departure, some weeks later. Our little schooner, which Dad the inventor had designed, was to be launched. I left abruptly. I did not even think of saying goodbye to the girl.

"The inventor did not turn up, either at the launching or during the subsequent glorious weeks I spent aboard with the jolly crew, sailing where our whims and the winds took us. Every night another port, including resorts, every night ending at one of the houses on the waterfront.

"A golden haze enveloped my vision, and even my whole being. I hardly thought of Susanna. I might have felt some stirring when her face emerged at an odd moment.

"On my return, I heard that she was pulled from the well a few weeks earlier. An accident . . . .

"They buried her in her confirmation dress, the busker told me.

"She had come and asked him about me. He had told her that I'd left forever."

BOOK II

Chapter Thirteen — **Willy**

"Eight horses or forty men." The white legend on the cattle wagon spoke of the hungry battlefields, an impression which lurked behind the hubbub an outsider might have taken for gaiety. There were flowers, banners and the devil-may-care bearing the young men assumed to bolster up their spirits and for the sake of their kin, *'Galgenhumor'* — the boisterous gaiety which apparently springs from deep down, though our insides are held in an icy grip.

There are some forty wagons for the men and a Pullman for the officers. Mothers, sweethearts, fathers and sisters — people from many walks of life, welded together by a field-gray destiny — stand in groups, around the boys. The latter are both newcomers and the veterans who floundered in the Serbian mud. Many who lasted through a hundred campaigns remember their comrades whose limbs froze in the Burana, the blizzard from the Russian steppe.

The boys wear carnations in cap behind the badge bearing the initals F.J.I. (for Francis Joseph the First). The portrait of the octogenarian displayed everywhere, in the first upsurge of patriotic fervour, shows a stern and benevolent man. It was easy to see the old man, humbled by both age and sorrows, trying to avert disaster.

Two years earlier, in 1914, the boys were sent "to defend him", to avenge the deaths of the Crown Prince and his lady. After a short interlude of dispensing justice to the treacherous Serbs, it was thought, they would resume their former pursuits.

Those were the days of make-believe, of the resolve "to show Francis Joseph" and to keep the promise "We will be back before the leaves fall." The white-clad maidens reflected, in tear-soaked smiles, the words written by the flutterings of flags in a Morse of their own. "We'll be back before the leaves fall."

Now, that is all over. The young ones still cherish the thought of a heroic death. It never occurs to them that it could be the end. In some mysterious way, they will live on, not as in the Valhalla where the souls of heroes slain in battle find eternal bliss, but in the hearts of those left behind.

They dream of the death of a hero, a theme the poets have extolled throughout the ages. Anyway, of those who do not come back, *"Dolce et*

69

decorum est pro patria mori," says the padre — then he remembers that the crowd is not made up solely of the gentry and repeats, in wistful Hungarian, "It is sweet and honourable to die for the country."

The breeze subsided. The sun dominated a cloudless sky, yet failed to radiate the usual summer heat. A sensation of vaporousness — such as one can feel in the vicinity of swamps — pervaded the air; but there were no swamps in the neighbourhood, not in a radius of a hundred miles. It was as though the sun had seeped through vapour or a veil — the veil of dark forebodings. Many such days followed in the subsequent years. Not even the oldest inhabitants remembered anything like the phenomenon. The peasants said that the war, smoke and cannon fire, created it.

As erect as the old emperor stood the Hamiltons. From the rear, the old man and his son could have been taken for brothers, but for their clothing. Willy wore the uniform of a lieutenant of the local 32nd infantry regiment, and the father, his broad shoulders tapering to a narrow waist, a gray tweed hunting outfit. Soldierly bearing apart, they had little in common with Francis Joseph the autocrat and disciplinarian.

The Hamiltons could have worn the toga of ancient Rome, their features fitted into — would have been familiar in — the senate of the eternal city. Francis Joseph, had he donned the toga, would have stood out as the retired Teutonic mercenary.

At the approach of the appointed hour, Willy entered the carriage and came to the window. Underneath stood a dismal little island, two of his younger brothers, Andrew and Eddy, back from school, and their friends Rade and Itzig. Andrew and Rade were both aged fourteen and the others one year younger. Old Hamilton rested his hand on Itzig's shoulder.

The little town, a honeycomb overflowing, brought all its warmth to the boys of the 32nd infantry, the home regiment under marching orders.

There were women in white, little cotton dress or satin blouse underlining dark, silky, Hungarian eyes. Long hair fell on delicate shoulders or was knotted into a Greek twist. The Hamilton boy did not notice the longing looks from the women. Bold or hesitant, they would have come at a mere glance, but the Hamiltons remained a forbidding entity.

The boy looked like a Hamilton — but for his fair hair and slaty distant eyes which were those of Brydie Costigan. On occasions, mostly at times of stress, they transfigured his face into the face of his mother. His mind was on his beloved Blanca. She had not come. The gap between them could not be bridged.

In olden times the poor were raised to share thrones. In the nineteenth century, the lower classes became a constant tributary to the peerage, and princesses ran away with their dancing instructors or gypsy fiddlers. Blanca Schönfeld came from an orthodox Jewish home, a world of taboos with customs as zealous as those of the Moslems.

"They don't guard their women with the yashmak. Their rigid rites and clannish isolation are just as effective. Such were the qualities that held Ahasuerus from merging with others."

He could think only of her black eyes, so deep in their sockets that they always seemed shaded. Her profile might have served as model for the Egyptian reliefs at Karnak. The uncanny fingers of the ancient craftsmen had carved the contours to catch the sun. So her profile — he shut his eyes as if forcibly to retain the vision — appeared to him to reflect light.

'My little rose of Hebron,' he mused, while he nodded assent to his father's last minute advice.

For a long time, he had sensed embers smouldering behind her slow movements and gestures — and her eyes which also moved slowly, as though deliberating. Then at the river a month ago, as the bells sounded the Angelus from the distant Franciscan monastery, he had discovered the elemental force and stood in awe before it. With anguish in his heart, he had felt that — unless the fire could be fed all the time — it would destroy her.

Late last night, he went again to meet her on the bridge that spans the River Glossy. His heart was pounding with the fear that she would not be able to sneak out of the house. The plane trees seemed to embrace each other across the water. The darkness, though deep, was not oppressive. A small lighted window at the mill, two score yards upriver, seemed to stress the darkness around, while the lazy river cradled its oblong reflection and twisted and broke it up.

Into his mind came fragments of a ballad about the mill and the river which flowed under his feet. The miller's wife swears fidelity to her husband. The Glossy will flow uphill before she disgraces him while he is away in Bosnia with the footsloggers of the county, the King's own 32nd infantry regiment . . . .

Willy leaned on the parapet. A solitary frog croaked. He felt a light touch on his arm. The small hand caressed him for a while, then found its way into his own.

"I shall take you to Vienna," he said. "Eventually, you will study medicine, as befits a revolutionary. You will be taciturn as today and dress as today. Thus, you will differ from the rebels from Warsaw or Scutari, short-haired girls, tempestuous and wearing high-necked Russian blouses. Attractive — but you're different, little Hebron rose."

As she did not speak he asked, in his reflective Hamilton way, whether she doubted his words.

She did not doubt his words, but fate. Persecution throughout the ages had implanted doubt towards long-term planning. Memories of the race and of the family going back merely a few generations — their life in the Ukraine and along the tortuous path till they had settled in Hungary — suggesting pitfalls at every step, the knowledge crystallised that planning a long time ahead never works.

The gentle pressure of his hand reminded her that he was waiting for an answer. At last she spoke, but her diffident voice disclosed that she could not define her thoughts. "Won't your father object?" she said.

"Dad, a man of magnificent impulses, is uncritical of anything genuine. He will help." After a while, he added: "Nor does Dad suffer from any class-consciousness. Once, I heard him say that the Hamiltons belong to no one stratum. We belong to all, to the wide world — to this broad and alien world."

After another pause, he went on in a voice that sank to a whisper, as though to keep in tune with the all-pervading silence: "Crowned heads, often deposed ones from the Balkans, mingled with travelling players in the rambling house. At least once, the winged words 'one king, one gypsy' came true. To this day some remember the night — the night of the big race-meeting at Fridenau. When the bookies wept, the celebration was at its height.

"At the table, more by chance than by Dad's wisdom, Ranoné sat between the Prince of Wales and the deposed king of the Serbs, or some other discarded puppet of Balkan intrigue. She was hardly more than a girl. Around the oval face, in harmony with its colouring, nestled the blue-black frame of her glossy hair — 'As if she had fed on corn, like the Hamilton horses before Tattersalls,' remarked the prince. 'I'll put you back on the throne,' he said, a friendly gesture towards a genial fellow-man. Contemporary opinion held the prince a most astute diplomatist whose generosity and seeming eccentricities always served his ends.

" *'La mort Socratique,'* replied the Serb with a twisted smile, as he stroked Ranoné's wrist. Thus the story goes — she enchanted them all," concluded Willy.

He kissed Blanca. The parted lips were cool and did not respond. He felt that sorrow, like icy hands, overspread her ardour and his.

He spoke again, in a voice that was louder but husky with emotion. "Stay at home till I return, Blanca. Don't let us burn the bridge."

She shrugged. "The flood after you," she said.

'But she has not come to the train.' Willy felt desolate.

At the shrill whistle of the non-coms., the soldiers scramble into their wagons. Tears, a last embrace, whispered encouragement, in some hearts the echo which seemed to mock: " . . . . back before the leaves fall."

The old man scans the boy's face at the window and slowly, under the impact of memories, the face of the boy fades into the face of the beloved wife. As if the old man is groping for strength, Itzig feels the grip tighten, and the hand grow heavy, on his shoulder.

Up goes the song, clear above the sizzle of steam and the clatter of wheels —

> 'How the six wheels of the steam engine
> glitter, glitter, glitter.
> On it travel to war
> the lads of the Thirty-two,
> poor ones, poor ones, poor ones.
> Don't cry, maidens from Lake Town.
> We'll yet come back to you
> one day, some time 'r never.'

The little island of the Hamiltons breaks up. Abruptly, the old man raises an arm. "Salve," he calls out, but is barely audible above the clamour. The boys race along the platform, dodging the waving bystanders. The coach awakes in Willy; he shouts instructions, about style and breathing, to the racing boys. The spindly-legged Itzig falls out; but Eddy, Andrew and Rade race on for another twenty or thirty yards, before giving in, the station building some hundred yards behind.

The engine belches a streak of black smoke. Snatches of the song come faintly —

> 'Don't cry, maidens from Lake Town.
> · · ·   · · ·   · · ·   · · ·   · · ·   · · ·
> one day, some time 'r never.'

The train changes into a toy in the distance before it vanishes around the bend.

Small groups of people pass by the boys, who sit down on the embankment waiting for the old man. As always, he is erect. Yet, there is a change, something intangible, as if his gait has lost its purpose.

Other groups follow them. A sorry procession trudges towards the town.

Chapter Fourteen
Blanca

"You know, well enough, what those Goyims want from you," said her father, while Blanca clutched the pink postcard. A few lines saying that he was well, the only message the censor permitted from the front.

The joy was overshadowed, for a while, by the bitterness that welled up in her breast at her father's words. Always assuming the worst! Could he not, for once, keep quiet? Did he not want to see his daughter happy? Were customs more important than her happiness?

The father said no more; but there he stood, an old testament prophet, his small, clear, blue eyes unflinching and resting on her as if he knew that rebellion went on inside her.

She stood his gaze, her dark eyes languid, unruffled by the ferocity in his. As though responding to something in him which went down to his roots, the mainstay of his illusions — the aggregate of his core which shaped his thoughts — she spoke slowly, in the lucid words and rounded sentences of one who thought all the time of the subject.

"Wouldn't we be happier without our rules and taboos, if our Gideon and the Maccabeans had been less heroic, if we had been absorbed by numerically bigger peoples? Had we been less resilient in the Diaspora, then we would not have been the scapegoat throughout the ages; our trail would not have been soaked in blood — there might have been no trail at all."

While she spoke, the blood mounted in the old man's face. His arm twitched, as though with the urge to strike the girl. She expected the blow but it changed into a small gesture of despair at the end of his strident words, "And my own blood telling me this — after a lifetime of struggle with Goyim and Jew alike, while the latter takes the whip lying down!"

Her words had touched the nerve-end of doubts — doubts the fanatic in him had shunned. Now, there was no escape. He hissed, "You speak the words of the Goyim you're after. Before, the gentry got our women by force or with gold. Today, they corrupt them with speech. Diaspora, taboo — words you never heard me say." As he uttered them his words lost some of their harshness, on his recollection that violence inside the family had always bred more trouble, but he remained unbending.

The last shred of filial piety compelled her to lower her eyes before the patriarch. Yet, she was unbeaten. The revolt went on underneath.

The tension abated, at the dinner-table, with the expression of the various emotions of members of the family including the oldest sons. Married and living in other parts of the country (like the three elder daughters), the pair had come on a visit.

After thirty years in Hungary, the mother — dark and, unlike Blanca, hefty — still retained traces of her soft native Russian. What she gathered from the girl's words recalled her own youth. She had defied elders as tyrannical as her husband, but the long weary trail, and the arrival of children had worn down resistance, transmuting rebellion into the docility of the yoked beast.

The two youngest children, pupils in the fifth and second forms at the lyceum, the monastery school of the Piarist monks, felt that the onslaught could have been directed against them too. Suddenly, these boys thought that the gap between Jews and gentiles — giving rise to the hush that fell on the Jews' approach, whispers behind their backs and even open hostility, at times when the word Jew was spoken in an accent unmistakably denoting all evil — was perhaps created by the Jews themselves. It came to them as a revelation that humiliation at the hands of gentiles was not the inevitable, inscrutable, way of nature. The Jews were at fault.

Blanca's words stirred them all. She gave shape to the vague and formless in their thoughts. The response was agreement varying in shade from the grudging to the eager — though unspoken, in the case of the eldest sons. Men on the threshold of middle life, they appreciated her emotions, but bitter experience had taught them that — whatever the cause of the hate — it was deep-rooted, complex, intangible, immensely strong. It had come down through the ages and would not abate if the Jew abandoned his ways (a miracle in itself, if it could be attained).

The desire to lose or hide the stigma Judaism stamped on him led to queer behaviour, antics of all kinds to escape hatred. Crudeness and cunning were employed against hostility in the fight for survival, efforts ranging from appeasement, through hatred, to violence.

The two oldest sons had lost, in the struggle, every vestige of youthful idealism akin to their sister's. She was just going through the initial phase, the phase of appeasement towards a hostile world. Comprehension as well as the rebuff experienced could be read in their sullen faces. They sat there, heads bowed and tongues weighed down by the inability of simple cattle-dealers — the lack of words to voice abstractions — and the knowledge of what instinct had told them from the start, when the quiet dark eyes had dared the patriarch. No words, however convincing, would avail to convince her.

The two inarticulate elder brothers knew in their hearts that the credulity of men craves sensations and beliefs, that accusation wants a scapegoat for wrongs more than a remedy and that the clamour for *autos-da-fé* and baiting of the weak contributes more towards persecution than any trait or weakness the Jew may possess. There was, also, the venom produced by frustrated ambitions and, simply, the hatred which looks for a target. The Jew was near.

All this lived in them, inexpressible, far behind the machinery of the spoken word.

The rebellion seethed behind Blanca's lowered eyes. "I can see a hunted look in some Jewish friends of mine," she recalled hearing Willy say. Warmth spread through her and the tension eased as the lean boyish face appeared to her mind's eye. The low timbre of his voice, slow and deliberate on each word, overcame adverse feelings. He was never emphatic, like others. Nor did he try to convince her, as did other men she met. His lofty ideas fired her thoughts.

She felt as though he was sitting beside her. Only with an effort could she refrain from extending a hand to guard the illusion.

"There will be no fear for your children — our children," he corrected. "They won't have to look behind their shoulders."

The diffused glow of the oil-lamp lulled her doubts. God, will it come true . . . She read again the familiar words of the pink field postcard. Then, unaware of the move, she tucked it into her blouse.

Still in communion with the presence, she heard the vesper-bell. She lived again the memorable spring evening. "Alkony" — the Hungarian word for dusk — "means crepuscule. Both the Hungarian and French words denote the melancholy aspect of dusk. Yet, don't you think," he asked her, "the words do not tally?"

She had recognised the steps — the beat of his footfalls which she could distinguish from amidst a marching regiment — as he came up from behind, then stopped to speak the slow, reflective, words.

She was at a loss. "Alkony means crepuscule . . . ." ran through her mind. She had no French but knew that he was right — as right he would be, whatever or whenever he spoke. She looked up, then her gaze roamed on to the water, the bridge a hundred yards up river and, beyond, where the mill barred a view of the vast Hungarian plain.

She hardly dared to speak, lest he noticed the emotion his words had induced. Her breast heaved. They had never spoken before. They had met in the street, almost daily. She had seen him crossing the bridge many an evening, at times taking a path along the river at the bottom of her father's garden. That night, though she had known he would come and speak to her, she was overwhelmed with frantic joy at his doing so. Yet, when she looked him fully in the face her eyes did not give her away, nor did the little movement of her hand — hardly more than half-hearted — that motioned him into the garden.

At the gate, he lingered as his eyes strayed towards the bridge which, through the mellow mimicry of dusk, merged into the puce background.

"You hesitated," she said, while he was seating himself beside her on the rug which she spread wider to allow space for them both.

"I stopped to steady myself. I was . . . I am incredibly happy . . . A little while before I stepped onto the bridge, I made up my mind to speak to you. Then I lost heart. My steps dragged me across the bridge which changed, for me, into 'the bridge of sighs'. The austere wooden bridge under our harsher climate seems to me more apt a symbol of sorrow than the elaborate Venetian structure."

Hands interlocked behind his neck, he glanced at the sky. A pale crescent of the waxing moon stood high in the deep, cool, blue eastern sky fading towards the luminous west. Trees cast endless dim shadows under a tired sun nearing the horizon. The vesper-bell called to the faithful. Grass blades on one side reflected the sun and on the other the pale iridescence of the moon.

"A mood when miracles can happen," he said.

As if putting her feelings into words would amount to profaning them, she answered briefly.

For a while, neither spoke. Slowly the mauve twilight enveloped them.

"It may have a bearing on our meeting," he said at last, "In some odd way, inexplicable in words . . . . apart from the name Blanca. I recall the ballad about Donna Blanca by Heine. You know it?"

She shook her head.

Slowly, his voice just above a whisper, he spoke the German verse elaborating on it in Hungarian when he missed a line or stanza —

Donna Blanca met the dark-eyed youth in her garden, under a starry sky. They ambled and spoke. His words reflected the enchanted world around them. He told her of the stars, the lilac-scented night, the twitter of the birds and the magic spirit of the garden. She expressed pleasure but, whatever he said, she inevitably returned to mentioning the Jews she hated so much. Each time, the youth tried to divert her hate by bringing up a new theme. Each time, she reverted to her obsession.

They called Donna Blanca into the house. On parting, she asked the youth to come again. Upon which he answered, while he untied his horse, *"Ich bin der Sohn des weltberuhmten Rabbi, Israel von Saragossa"* — "I'm the son of the world-famed Rabbi Israel of Saragossa."

Willy echoed her sigh as they sat alone, under the starlit dome of heaven, with the little noises and stirrings of the night around them. "We must go," said Blanca. "I am happy — incredibly happy, as you said and I must guard it. It will be a vigil of" — she hesitated before she spoke the words — "of infinite joy." Then, in a low key, almost inaudibly, she added, "But, surely, it cannot last."

She touched his arm, pressed it slightly and went threading her way, in the dark, through the weeds and underbrush of an unkempt garden.

Slowly they walked off the bridge, along the path between river and gardens, leaving behind them the mill and the lock where the water sizzled as it pressed through cavities near the river-bed (the only sound far and wide). They walked as in a dream and as though led by a power at once within and outside them, whose interplay forged a communion that occurs only scantily during a lifetime. They were drawn slowly, inexorably, without the slightest jerk, their footfalls muffled by the lush grass.

Now, they were far out in the puszta. Here and there was an arbour of acacias grown to bind the soil of the expanse of Hungarian lowland. The sweet scent of the late blossoming held their hearts captive. In the distance, winding rows of both poplars and willows delineated the highway and the course of the river. A horse drowsing on all fours, or a cow in a half-sitting posture chewing the cud, added inexplicably to the sense of transience that hovered under the blinking stars.

Under an old acacia, he leans against the trunk, his hands resting on her waist. Her arms enfold him. The power that brought them here does not seem to cease. Unaware of either urge or decision, without a word, they lie at the foot of the tree in each other's arms.

Her maidenhood resists, giving him time to reflect on the possible damage to her. His desire flags. Her arms tighten round his neck. Scorching, through her clenched teeth, come the words "Do, darling" which whip up his desire.

Billowing red breakers assault his doubts, then a tidal wave of passion swamps the last vestige of them and blots out every thought.

Chapter Fifteen
Hamilton and His Friends

How luckless the mother
whose son is a cobbler.
She won't know at what hour
he'll drop into the glue-pot.

Bars of the above ragging song came jerkily, above the hammer-strokes, when Hamilton and Itzig entered the whitewashed and thatched peasant cottage, the boy's home in Hattyuliget Horditas Street (that was the name the rusty plate bore, anyway, though no one ever thought of it except as 'the Mount of the Frogs').

It was an old part of Lake Town where peasant cottages grudgingly gave way to some more northern structures which displayed, in the manner of the century's turn, a mixture of both Greek and Renaissance features blended under mock Gothic turrets, our eternal longing for beauty — for the original or for something different — running amok in the country builders' interpretation. And yet amongst the monstrosities one finds something unexpected, quaint, or even inspired, in spite of the mixed styles — just as, at times, American craftsmen can translate *Crime and Punishment* into a revue operetta and get away with it.

The cottage stood in a garden, a small arm of which stretched in front of the house with a few bushes of yellow autumn roses planted, on his holiday before the war, by Oscar (Itzig's oldest brother who had been sent, before the turn of the century, to Munich — then to Paris — to study painting at Count Esterhazy's expense).

The hammer-strokes as well as the song bewailing the fate of the cobbler ceased when Hamilton, preceded by Itzig, passed through the low doorway. Hand resting on the boy's shoulder, the old man had to bend his head to enter. Even so, the faded lintel was barely above his shoulder.

On the right of the door, two small windows shafted the westering sun, above pots of geraniums. Under the sun-rays, the heads of three cobblers bent over shoes, stretched and kept in place in their laps. Meanwhile, each man's fingers waxed the thread and pressed the needle perpendicularly through leather to be received and drawn, from underneath, by three fingers of the other hand.

Suddenly, all activities ceased and the three heads turned as Hamilton and Itzig came in. The odour peculiar to the cobbler's workshop hung in the air, in spite of the open windows and door. Kobie Borichaner the shoemaker — slight, oldish — sat facing the windows. Putting hammer and spikes on the low table before him, on top of various tools of the trade, he rose and quietly spoke the greeting customary in Hungary, "God's might brought you." Hamilton's sorrow was hardly obvious but Kobie Borichaner was aware of it as, in a mutual friendship from childhood, one often knows the other's feelings.

The door facing the windows opened with a little whine. Itzig's mother, a slight woman, descended the two steps which led up to the communicating door between kitchen and lower lying workshop.

The black garb of the peasant woman assumed some distinction under the silvery hair that crowned a high forehead above dark, placid eyes. She had brought a chair from the living-room — 'clean room' — for Hamilton. With her pinafore she wiped the highly polished chair, a purely symbolic gesture of respect towards the guest.

She took in both hands his proffered one then, seized by a sudden impulse, bent down and kissed it. Hamilton sat down, his thoughts elsewhere. Inobtrusively, the woman withdrew. Her placid eyes caressed the sitting man before she mounted the two steps, somehow laboriously.

The shoemaker, too, scrutinised the guest above the steel-rimmed spectacles on the tip of his nose (which lent him a slightly comical aspect). The work resumed. With nimble fingers, the journeymen waxed the thread and plied the needles. Again, the master drove wooden nails into the sole of the upturned shoe and he gestured to the apprentice to resume singing "Unhappy is the mother . . . "

Hamilton sank into reverie amidst the bustle of the workshop, as he did at times when he felt in need of warmth. (This occurred with increasing frequency during the war years.)

Time and again, he remembered the scene he had witnessed in the early part of the war, when enthusiasm was still at its peak. After eleven o'clock, he was enjoying his *déjeuner à la fourchette;* the goulasch served on a small plate was very tasty that day.

At the neighbouring table, Jovanovits the lawyer rose slowly. Big manly tears rolled down his cheeks and hid in his black beard. He was among a number of professional men who met daily, at the inn, for their morning break. Around the wobbly table — wine, beer or food in front of them — some told anecdotes, or discussed current events across the brightly patterned table-cloth, while others glanced through the morning paper.

The lawyer rose heavily, for a second resting on his arms while he bent over the spread out paper as though fascinated. He could not turn his eyes from an article, an account from the front by a special correspondent, about the destruction wrought by our army amidst the Serbs — the devastation, houses levelled and the black spot where a village had stood before — vivid writing by a gifted reporter.

Slowly the lawyer turned and — while some of his companions looked aghast and others gaped — walked to the sink next to the bar and washed his eyes.

To some it may have occurred, before, that Jovanovits came of Serb stock. Nationalism, on the upgrade for generations, was really a platonic sentiment, pride in one's own nation, scorn — as against competitors — towards other nations around. It was not yet a question of race. Though the one who adopted us might even speak our language brokenly, he was one of us. No one had ever thought that the lawyer was not part of us. Popular because he was handsome, he was an upright man known as straight in his dealings. His companions were moved by the scene.

A young captain of the hussars, a regular soldier on sick-leave (his bandage covered a shot-wound), got up. He went over to the sink, stood behind Jovanovits whose shoulders shook in a spasm of renewed grief and, when the lawyer turned, he embraced him awkwardly — as we do the first time we embrace a lovely woman.

From our early childhood, we hear and read of historic events. The account of the young Jew's courage and the stations of the cross and its variations are perhaps drummed into us till we become weary of it all — as the Huguenot might feel about St. Bartholomew Night. Tamerlane's pyramid of skulls, or the crucifixion of the slave army for a hundred miles along the Appian Way, awakes our sympathy for but a short while if presented by a good writer — or even by the superb artist whose victims of the *autos-da-fé*, in their triangular headgear, are a most moving human document. Our sympathy is eased by the knowledge that it all happened long ago and couldn't happen again . . . .

Through chinks in his consciousness it came to Hamilton that, as the light faded, the journeymen got up and left. The apprentice soon followed.

Itzig's father went on with the work of nailing on soles. At his feet, Itzig sat on a three-legged stool with a large open book across his knees.

The woman came again and placed a tray with hot coffee and cups on the crowded work-bench, on top of a pile of tools, half-made shoes and calf-hide marked with white chalk. She moved almost soundlessly. Nor did she speak when she offered the coffee to Hamilton, who reached for it mechanically.

She lit the oil-lamp which hung, from a wire, in the middle of the room, and Oscar's painting of Dósza, king of the serfs, came to the fore between the windows facing the sun. The dark eyes, at once feverish and resigned, dominated the picture which — influenced by the Fauves — was a discord created from primary colours and moulded into unity by the deft hand of Oscar. The king of the serfs sat on his throne, a red-hot iron structure, the sceptre and orb in his hands — throne, crown and insignia made for the occasion, his execution, as implements of torture to mock the insurgents and as a deterrent to those who would rise.

His hair burnt away, beard and moustache singed, he sits tied to the

F

stake shaped as a throne and, with pagan Eastern equanimity, he endures suffering. The screaming colours reflected as highlights in the feverish eyes enhance the serenity of his face.

"Oscar's got it in his bones," said Hamilton, launching it out softly. "It's the suffering of ages and he is the perfect medium to convey it. His peasant king incarnates humanity in bondage, which he leads without personal ambition. So, at least, the painting appears to me. Here is the man who could not be bought off, with promises of wealth and safe conduct, to abandon his charge, the serfs.

"So the Hungarian poet, too, felt" — he pointed at the book on Itzig's lap which, as if by coincidence, lay open at 'The Welsh Bards' — "as one whose legacy is the cross carried by each generation and handed down through the ages. None save Arany could render the horror of sending the five hundred bards to the stake and the madness of King Edward.

"Before, I too enjoyed such poetry and paintings — the presentation more than the events they portrayed and the actual message. My forebears were neither persecuted nor in bondage. There was no echo in me, no sympathetic magic.

"The long Red Cross trains with the sick and the wounded, the war-crippled in the street, first brought it home and conditioned me . . . And now that Willy has left I feel the jolt, though that too will be swallowed by my humdrum life . . . "

Hamilton's words petered out. After a short pause, Kobie took up the word. He spoke in accents of quiet resignation and frowned as he concentrated, eyes half closed, "You don't say it in so many words, yet it sounds as if you meant 'Why all this?'

"There is no answer — only platitudes or, at best, small coins of wisdom.

"My own autocratic faith, the notions of free will, predestination, powers at work — in the form of plagues and wars — to keep an equilibrium so that plants, vermin, beast and man do not overrun the earth, and the materialistic doctrine which finds explanations for everything in the economic field are but stages in our development. Notions to explain phenomena which soon turn out no more than explaining away things.

"You abandoned your scholarly endeavour based on the work of Bojuy — because it struck you as too fictional — when Einstein published his paper, thinking on similar lines, and resignedly termed it 'Zeitgeist'.

"Years ago, I thought the medieval mind persists because, being at sea, it needs to hold onto something even if it is an overturned boat — such as the anthropomorphic god. But rational man is just as much at sea, without the aid of the overturned boat.

"I know that, to a great extent, I echo you, but there it is . . .

"The flies might know every crevice, every brushstroke of Oscar's picture — but not its meaning. So is our perception inadequate. We just scratch the surface."

As a rule, Kobie distrusted much theory. His words subsided though he moved his lips a little, as we do when — lonely — we speak the name of a faithless lover.

"Above all, we are old and spent," he added, "our functions sluggish. They don't nourish an unimpaired intellect. That casts a veil on our eyes that makes us just as wrong as when we were young men driven by urges and gave not a second to reflective thought."

The slow, almost monotonous voice brought Hamilton back to his surroundings. When, at last, he began to gather Kobie's words, he nodded. Then he spoke haltingly, more to himself.

So far as he was concerned, he knew that age had not diminished his creative powers. He still heard the voice he had first heard — or had first become aware of — in his youth, in Vienna, while pressing his chest against the marble edge of the table in the Café Mozart. He felt uneasy about words he spoke drying up. Yet, such a feeling of unease, coupled with emotions of every kind, events and experiences, only helped the voice to be heard more and become more articulate.

He once heard it above the booming of the Bora — the northern gale — as he sailed in his ketch off Sebenico, in Dalmatia, along the seal-headed rocks when the solution came to him about the aerodynamic forces produced by the body of the flying machine at which he had worked, on and off, for years.

With a small gesture he brushed aside the blasphemous entreaties and hand-wringing of Antonio the skipper while, at the first sign of the icy gale, the fishermen raced to the shore. As the Bora lashed the yacht and grew in intensity, he tied himself to the mast. In the waning yellow-gray light, mathematical symbols gathered on the oily paper, while the yacht danced like a nutshell on the waves.

For a long time the fishing folk talked about the exploit, which visibly pleased him when the skipper mentioned it. The answer "One of the roots of creative thought is exhibitionism" seemed just as puzzling (to Antonio) as Hamilton's words and actions at other times.

He heard the voices in other places, at the stock exchange where men stalked with the faces of hungry wolves, through the vapour of sweat, drive and frustration, in times of crisis or the wildest bidding, and on the racecourse at the moment of a close finish when the name of the winner went up from a thousand hoarse throats.

He heard it in the vicinity of the swamp where he supervised the draining of marshes, according to a plan he had devised, canalising the water in newly dug straight channels, thus shortening the winding course of the sluggish river and hastening the outflow of water.

He heard it while grappling with administrative and legal questions which constituted the real bog through which one could not cut a straight channel — landlords' rights, tenants' rights, owners' rights, local politics. He found one solution when he heard the harsh and sweet lullaby a Dunyevac mother sang over the cradle. Then again, he heard the voice over the din of a brawl which broke out at the hostelry 'Kutyakaparo' — the nearest thing to a caravanserai in Middle Europe — along the highway which, in a rainy spring, merges into the puszta, the highway which saw the hordes of Huns, Mongols and Turks, and which slowed down the armies of the Tsar when they came, in the rainy autumn of '49, to quell the Hungarian revolt.

Hamilton sat over his pint of wine, the produce of the surrounding sandy waste, and his calculations — the latter taking shape because he heard the voice in the silence which resembled the quiet before the storm — and showed no interest in the shindy that broke out suddenly, to be over in minutes.

The peasant lad who thought himself slighted by a word was an inspired fighter. He kicked, hit with his fists and threw bottles and mugs, almost simultaneously, and cleared the bar parlour in next to no time while the Kutyakaparo's landlord and staff ducked behind the counter.

The stocky lad approached the quietly boozing Hamilton, his spirits still high. Perhaps a sense of gallantry tempered his glory, as he did not pounce on the sitting man but, stopping two paces away, requested him to leave. Was it that Hamilton felt it below his dignity to fight at his age — he was already past sixty — or was it stratagem? He himself could not to this day account for it. He rose slowly, as if he wanted to leave, then, in passing, he grabbed the broad-shouldered peasant. The latter went as limp as if in the embrace of the Virgin of Nuremberg, was carried to the door in a few strides and shared the fate of his victims who, by now recovered, followed the proceedings through closed windows.

Hamilton returned to the table, wrote down in his usual clear hand his instructions to the lawyers on the subject of owners' rights (with which he had grappled for weeks), drank the rest of his wine and placed some silver on the table. He then left unhurriedly, the voice receding into the distance.

He thought of events and sensations — the more active, the better — neither as mere stimulants nor as the rotting apple on the writing-desk of the German poet, but as tying down part of his being (as he termed it) to let his senses perceive the voice.

What was the voice like? Only at times was it musical, as deep and vibrant as the voice of a violoncello, then again like a spinet's when — for no apparent reason — it sounds at night.

At times, the musical sound was only part of the sensation, for example on an autumn night when the moon took a trip behind racing clouds and the scent of juniper flew with the wind.

God knew why he remembered a night spent along the River Dnieper where the horses drew the wheat-laden barge upriver, in front of the manor, and the host spoke about the socage which still persisted in Russia. He remembered the yellow hair of the hostess ruffled by the wind, and her white face silvery in the shade where it reflected the dazzling white satin shawl. Miura was her name, and her movements and far-away look — in short, her aura — spoke of the joy of living, the vigour of the Russian waste, at the time of his stay.

He identified the experience with the outcry of the Russian poet, a cry in the night echoing over the swamp, then through the sieve of the past. It seemed to him that it was the voice, but the same voice, which might have inspired Mr Turgenev. When translated into his own idiom of rigid mathematical thought it began to glow with the hues of the Russian sunset, the woman's bridled passion giving it intensity, then the thought became indistinct and finally ran into sand — like the Turgenev character who fought for the serfs and was then derided by them.

The voice also appeared as the demented scent, at dusk, of an Anatolian rose garden where he sat with a student friend of his youth, or as the Hungarian gypsy music of which no one had yet found words to describe the rousing quality and infinite sadness and overtones — the sublimation of all a race lived to see down the ages.

Only the strange music, the harmonies and contending passages have the power to portray the two sisters, two flowers of the village, who both yearned for happiness. The one is now being led to her wedding, the other was taken quietly to her grave some time ago. The music warns the mother not to grieve for the dead one, nor to rejoice in the fate of the other. Only the poetry of the music can ensure the trueness of the tale, words always fail. Such music never failed to stir Hamilton to his deepest.

He stalked the voice, too. He travelled in distant foreign lands where they produced food and drink of unknown composition, and where the women lied in a strange tongue.

He travelled in England to draw on the energy stored up behind the slow-moving and effortless speech consisting of set expressions and colloquialisms, often enough answered by one's questioner; "Nice day, isn't it?" or "How are you, quite well, aren't you," even if you were just mourning your wife's death, to spare you the effort to think up an answer.

For the opposite reason, he liked to travel in Germany where everything is emphatically explained and men spend themselves to do so. He remembered the Hungarian doggerel —

> 'Scholarly race is the German,
> thanks to Grandius,
> Because love-making itself
> is theory with them.'

Behind animated discussion which he could stimulate and bring to white heat, the voice rose, like instruments in an orchestral concert, from the tender flute to the rousing contra-violin.

In a God-forsaken little township of Lower Austria, at the height of a discussion at the inn where the stale smell of beer and tobacco-smoke promised no balm for the remorse of the morning after the night before, he heard the voice after the departure of the last mendicant friar who had sneaked in for a drop of schnapps.

It was a melting adagio, harmonies and counterpoint, with the infinite magic of music. As the last guests left, Hamilton wrote feverishly.

The bull-necked barman wiped the counter and a hefty maid put the chairs upon the tables. Hamilton wrote by the light of an oil-lamp. The maid lingered, as if waiting for a word to make her stay, then she left, following the barman, while Hamilton remained unaware of his surroundings.

Chapter Sixteen
Itzig and His Schoolfellows

The Piarist monastery, on a hill, overlooked the lake from a height of about one hundred and fifty feet. It sprawled over the crest of the hill. A huge corrridor paved with granite slabs led to the dining-hall, kitchen and now disused classrooms.

In the middle of the ground-plan stood the well-decorated main staircase, which led to a better lit corridor above. Here an almost friendly mood prevailed within the ancient walls. A fresco at the east end of the corridor represented Ignatius Loyola amidst a holy assembly. Most likely by chance, the artist had depicted St. Ignatius as a haughty grandee. The painting fadged with the rather impersonal baroque interior.

This floor housed the not too austere private quarters of the monks — in olden times, cells — and their charges, the sons of the well-to-do of the country, the ennobled bourgeoisie and the aristocracy. Just after 7.30 in the morning, both monks and students rushed to the chapel, on the west side, where they were joined by students from the town and surrounding villages who did not board at the Piarist collegium. After the morning service, the students formed a procession. Led and shepherded by the monks, they set out for the new school — the gymnasium — a four-storeyed building endowed with both Renaissance and baroque features. This building, too, stood above the lake. In its grounds, the pupils of denominations other than Catholic whiled away the time with games and peripatetic studies, while the Catholics worshipped. At the advent of the procession they stood on both sides and allowed 'the church-goers' to file inside the building, then followed them — rowdily, as befitted 'heathens and heretics'.

Everybody was already in his seat when Itzig entered, engrossed in a book.

Three rows of desks faced the dais with the master's desk. Itzig sat down at a desk in the third row. He took the much fingered history book from amongst his books, the rest of which he automatically put in the locker, and went on reading his book on astronomy. Life around him, the banter and ribaldry, appeared as through a haze. He felt the smallness of his environment, his soul shed the limitations, reached into the infinite and soared amongst planets and their satellites in nebulae.

His imagination outstripped them in the thousands of miles per second race. Life around him registered only to the extent that he knew, after years of bitter experience, when to dodge a wet sponge or a kick or — if caught unawares — how to bear pain or discomfort mutely.

The lofty, whitewashed walls bore but one image: the crucified Jesus, above the master's desk. The well carved, painted, thirty-inch image against the bluish-white wall was designed to instil devotion — a feeling which, if inspired, did not last with the lively breed.

On the wall at the right of the master's desk there was a reversible blackboard, easily shifted as desired. On the left — next to the door — stood a huge, square, wickerwork basket for waste paper and other refuse. No one knew why the sixth form* was provided with such a big refuse box. Some wits maintained that the whole Rombach Utca — the Jewish quarter in Budapest — could find room in it.

The master rarely entered before a quarter past eight. So, the animated scene went on, uninhibited. Some repeated lessons aloud, others argued or told jokes amidst laughter. With a flair for showmanship, Hitch jumped on his desk and eyed Andrew Hamilton. Under the impression that he had detected Hitch's art in the vivid phallus symbol — realistically drawn across the illustration of the three Graces in his textbook on antiquity — Hamilton had waved a fist and abused him.

Hitch now declaimed nobly with Cicero. *"Quo'sque tandem abutere, Catilina . . . ."*

Hamilton did not point accusingly at Hitch but tore his shirt open, as if to encourage a would-be assassin to shoot him in the chest. He displayed a martyred face while Hitch continued the Latin tirade.

Cicero might have envied the nobly resonant timbre of Hitch's oratory. Hamilton himself was no mean actor. With a sweeping gesture, which ended in a thud as his fist landed against his chest, he stood there for seconds in utter dejection — a familiar move of the great Waldemar Psylerden, idol of the films' heroic days.

Slowly, Hamilton bent his head and dropped his fist. Suddenly, he raised his head. His lips pursed and eyes narrowed, his face spoke of resolution. In two bounds, he reached the refuse box and lifted the lid. He went through the motions of the magician conjuring up or spiriting away a white rabbit, then hid himself in the box.

For a minute, nobody stirred. Hamilton had stolen the show. But it was not yet over. Rade, in the second row of desks, signalled to the class to stay silent. Then he tiptoed to the door, opened it and closed it with a bang. He dragged his shuffling steps to the desk, amidst the chorused welcome of the pupils on their feet. *"Laudetur Jesus Christus."*

The lid of the box went up, revealing a scared face. The boy looked round, spat contemptuously from the box when he realised they had fooled him, and vanished again. Nothing happened for minutes. Every

---

*Not equivalent to English Sixth Form, the Sixth in this case is succeeded by Seventh and Eighth Forms.

eye rested on the box; even Itzig showed mild interest, while his mind dwelt on the phenomena of the planets and their satellites.

At 8.15 Blanar the stocky young monk, the history master, arrived. Briskly, he made his way to the desk, opened the class register and asked the name of anyone missing. Nobody was missing, not even Hamilton. He signed the sheet.

Though he was invisible, Hamilton's presence made itself felt. From here came a chuckle and from there a guffaw which, in one case, was smothered into a spasm of coughing to disguise it. Prods in his back and ribs urged Shilling to declare Hamilton (his neighbour) missing, but they were resisted, leaving him with black and blue marks.

This was the young monk's first term. He hid his lack of experience behind a somewhat forced joviality, which did not deceive the expert eye of the class, but they had learnt that uncertainty could stand up well when confronted by adversity. The young master, by no means a fool, could counter trouble and root it up with a severe hand, as he had already shown on one occasion.

Expectancy began to subside into lying in wait. However, the refuse box was no longer the centre of interest. While some recounted salient features or principal names of the lesson, on Caligula's reign, others weighed the chances of being called on. The master slowly turned over the pages of his notebook. As he was doing so he kept on the *qui vive* for a sound or some other indication of a weak spot to pounce upon in that complex patchwork, the class. He may have felt something in the air. Slowly his hand caressed his forehead and he threw a casual glance at the class. The soft glance was but a sharp scrutiny.

Rade did not expect to be called. At the last lesson and at the one before that, the master had called on him. A joyful anticipation of the developments in the refuse box affair contended with his day-dreams about a stamp of the Vatican State. The stamp would be the highlight of his collection, if only he could raise the money to buy the collection (now on sale) which contained it! Plans not unlike those of western adventurers eager to acquire idols of Bhudda with eyes of diamond — though neither idols nor eyes were on sale — crossed his mind.

"Rade," the master said, but had to speak again before there was any response.

The complexity of Rade's thoughts were yet deepened by the master's call. He was caught unawares. He had given the first part of the lesson a cursory reading. He remembered a phrase written in a bold hand, by the previous owner of the book, about Caligula's appointing his four-year-old horse Consul — and that was all. Only for a second did his face display adverse emotions. The fingers of his right hand harrowed his fair mane as the powerfully built, short fellow looked round for help. Finding none, he stepped from the desk and, with a desperado's slouch, walked along the passage between desks and windows to the rostrum. He stopped at the blackboard. Marshalling his scanty knowledge, he waited for a cue.

The master looked at him attentively and made an urging gesture.

"Well, Sir, I don't know how to begin."

"You mean you can't think of the first word," said the master.

Rade sensed a pitfall but, on the other hand, did not want to reject the chance of a helping hand. He nodded, hoping to gain time.

"The . . . " the master blurted out and beamed. The class laughed spontaneously, perhaps seizing the opportunity to break the tension which, though lessened, was still in the air.

The master, who often thought himself a wit, swallowed contentedly. He turned benevolent eyes on Rade and, with an easy question on Rome, helped the boy to build a picture. Rade also remembered books he had read on the ancient world. Eventually, in cumbersome sentences, he created something novelists like to term local colour. He threw in here and there one of the few carefully husbanded facts and made a big show of the event he referred to as "Caligula's folly", the horse created Consul. He returned to the event and dislayed a propensity for both philosophy and ethics and would have rambled on, if the master had not cut him short with a witty word which no one caught though they sensed it was a laughing matter.

A belly-laugh arose from the last desk on the right. Another echoed it, from the opposite side, followed by Hitch's whinny. The rest joined in. The master did not laugh. He perceived the false note on which the gaiety had started. Though his severity thawed, he remained serious. Later, he referred to the performance as "studied merriment". His raised hand silenced it.

"Rade," he said, "I must admit you nearly got away with it, but for the philosophy, when you ran out of material. You may have read *Quo vadis* and other books on antiquity and remembered snatches of my Tuesday lecture. At times you were out by hundreds of years, but what are a few centuries between friends? Go back to your desk and we'll forget about the affair."

Rade thanked him and hurried happily to his place. An attentive class awaited further developments. They nearly forgot the refuse box.

"No, the philosophy was not in keeping with the age. What do you think, Borichaner?"

Nobody but a newcomer like the monk Blanar would have called Itzig by his surname. The boy rose — or attempted to, but something held him back. He thought it a practical joke, gathered all his strength and stood up. A sharp tearing sound accompanied the motion. His trouser-seat remained stuck to the wooden bench, exposing a semi-circular shape of white underpants. All eyes converged on the spot. Homeric laughter ensued.

The master suppressed a smile. He realised at once that some wag had poured quick-drying glue on the bench. He also saw tears in Itzig's eyes and sensed that they were not only tears of humiliation.

"Whoever did it, I'm not interested in his name but I expect him to pay for the damage. I believe that all of you know the war has created such conditions that it isn't easy to come by cloth. Nor do I think that Borichaner comes of a family made rich by the war. If the man in question cannot pay, a collection will be held in the class. If it is insufficient, I'll pay the rest. Hitch, please deal with the matter and report to me tomorrow."

Back at the desk, he lectured on the aftermath of Caligula's reign till the bell announced the end of the lesson.

When Blanar left, excited groups discussed the events. Others rushed to the refuse box, to witness Hamilton's emergence. He felt like "the fakir sealed in a sack and buried for a decade".

Blanar's move started the row which began in the pause between the history and German lessons. The laconic Hitch wrote out the list of names during the break, as if tacitly assuming the collection was necessary. Nerves keyed up by the events of the first hour, some protested and their number grew while the pupils entered the classroom and settled down at their desks. "It's just not right that we should pay instead of the fellow who did it."

The September sun shone unabated, the heat was great. On other days — even on less hot ones — the dreary German lesson dragged and dragged. The minutes moved like the feet of weary camels crossing the desert. The class languished in the monotony. Now, hard words lashed at the one for whom they all had to suffer. Accusation followed accusation. Names were mentioned. By far the quietest was Shilling, who as a rule never failed to act as ringleader. Hitch observed the proceedings behind a mask of swotting. With the advent of the master, the clamour changed to a sizzling, ready to flare up at any moment.

By now Itzig, immersed in his book, was again in his seventh heaven. He would have remained seated, but the forceful reminder of his neighbour brought him to his feet.

Mr Stoll the master was a seedy, bespectacled individual aged about forty and tallish, his thinning hair fair behind a greenish-gray sheen. He was not a monk, but one of the secular masters the state attached to the school. He went to the desk, sat down, fumbled with the register and, all the time, avoided looking at the class.

His eyes blinked nervously behind glasses which mirrored the windows. When he faced the class, one could see that Mr Stoll suffered from a tic.

Shilling's quietness had not escaped the hawk eye of Hitch. The latter decided that the culprit was Shilling and acted by passing him the list of names and whispering that he must put down his contribution as the first. He looked meaningly at Shilling, who reddened to the roots of his hair, puzzled as to who could have given him away. He had believed that nobody knew. "Why I?" came the whisper from his anger-distorted lips, but his daggers-drawn look met only a measured smile from Hitch.

Both hostile whisper and angry face attracted the master's attention.

"What's up, Shilling?" he shouted.

"No--- nothing, Sir," stammered Shilling, now standing.

"Nothing?" bellowed the master. "Yet you look quite beside yourself and this damn' class sounds like a beehive. I'll show you."

The boys listened to the angry words, in the hope of a spectacle. In the back corner on the right, Brezima the cheer-leader and his cronies abandoned their quiet poker game, for the moment, and looked towards the dais.

"Let's see whether your German is as bold as your behaviour," the master continued, his tone an octave lower.

The mild interest flagged, the boys relapsed into their abandoned activities. Shilling's rendering German into Hungarian or, as it happened to be in this case, Hungarian into German, was a much too familiar scene to promise much fun. He stayed in his place, turned the pages laboriously to find the text in question, then — by way of a call for help in an emergency — touched the shoulder of the boy in front of him. The helper took no chances. He wrote down the German words, keeping abreast with Shilling's reading which was akin to slow motion on the films:

"The ass of the Pope walked across the bridge . . . " Shilling's eyes took in the German words his classmate wrote and repeated. *"Der Esel des Pabstes ging über der B . . . . "* He could not read the word for bridge jotted down in a scrawl. He scowled and pushed his helper who, not understanding what the trouble was, pointed at the indistinctly written word.

"Ah," said the master, triumphantly, "you don't know the German for bridge — not even such a simple word — but you can hiss imprecations. Oh, *ja, natürlich . . . "* He often turned, in anger, to his native German.

At that moment his eyes fell on Itzig, who looked miles away. His mind, in reality, dwelt in that notable W-shaped group of stars — the constellation Cassiopeia.

"Itzig!" The master's sharp voice, supplemented by a push from behind, brought him to his feet.

"Well," said the master and, as no reply came from the boy, he added, "Bridge, didn't I say bridge?"

Itzig looked round for help. His eyes rested on the Latin words the boy in front of him had written in block letters. *PONS ASINORUM.*

"Bridge, Sir, of course, Sir," he said *"Pons asinorum."*

Pons asinorum — bridge of the asses! After a second's gasp from the class, the scene was drowned in laughter which grew in volume when those who had been wrapped up in their own activities joined in (on receiving information with regard to Itzig's words).

Anger blackened the master's face. Now, as always, he suspected affront — in the answer as well as in the subsequent gaiety. Again and again, waves of mirth swept the class, encouraged by the cheer-leader's belly-laughs and whinnies. The master's signal for silence failed. Only after frantic waving and shouts could he reduce the noise to such a level that he could address Itzig:

"You seem to think that we forgather here to make jokes, don't you? — jokes of such doubtful taste, at that — an assembly of professional humorists and funny men! You think that, don't you? Why don't you answer?"

Itzig stood there like a plaster cast draped with clothes, a strange scarecrow. His eyes were nearly shut, his cheeks and lips bloodless. The master's words poured over him, as in a dream. Hard words could not fully banish the planets and constellations. His thoughts harked back, after each whiplash of reproach.

"You're recalcitrant. Why don't you answer?"

"I don't know what to answer," pleaded Itzig.

"What were you thinking?" shouted the master.

"I thought of nebulae separated by distances the light can traverse in thousands of miles per second, the space so overwhelming that in comparison our affairs are of no importance. I thought of the planets and constellations . . . . "

The man felt the weight of the unhurried words but could not afford to lose the argument. "So you think that German is of no importance?"

Here another voice interposed, "German industry and superiority . . . . when our glorious ally fights a life and death struggle? Good men scorn them."

The master recognised the husky voice. "What did you say, Rade?"

The heavily built youth stood up ponderously. Sympathy for his friend's plight had prompted the spontaneous words. Once discovered, he decided to back him up squarely. "For hundreds of years, we've laboured under the German yoke. When he could not avoid uttering a German name Horvath, the retired history master, mimicked spitting, pulled out his handkerchief and wiped his mouth: A symbolic but telling act."

The master gasped. He remained silent. Only his frequent tic showed what went on inside him. Reaching for the register, he announced that he was going to make entries for insulting behaviour — the worst that could happen to a pupil, short of expulsion — by both Rade and Borichaner.

In the comparative silence, while he fumbled for a pen, a name was spoken from one of the rear benches. "Paldy." It had the effect of the toreador's red cloth. The man threw down the pen. A screech issued from his mouth, ahead of incoherent words.

The name 'Paldy' was a reference to an episode which occurred in the previous year, when Paldy boarded with Mr Stoll. On one occasion, the master found his middle-aged wife and the handsome youth in an ambiguous situation. The woman succeeded in persuading him that he had only imagined things, but some chance words of their little son re-awakened his doubts. The subsequent questioning of the five-year-old destroyed the edifice built by womanly guile.

The bloodshot face, the veins protruding like cords in Mr Stoll's forehead and the maddened turkey-screams met with approval. Amidst shouts and catcalls, Paldy's name was turned into a battle-cry. "Paal-dy-ee-ee," synchronised by a few, added colour to the show.

A thin voice shouted, "They sold the bed" — an allusion to the rustic wisdom which holds that after the woman is taken in adultery, they sell the sinful bed and things go on as before.

The Paldy incident was hushed up. Conferences were held behind closed doors but Paldy was not expelled. He changed his domicile and left at the end of the school year, with the warning not to return.

It was an unhappy coincidence that the Stolls had a new baby. Before he ever saw daylight, it was said that he was the image of Paldy. There is no need to stress that this was merely malicious talk. After reflection, one is justified in saying that such talk was not uncommon in little Hungarian towns.

Stoll could endure no more. He forgot his intention to enter Rade and Itzig — in the register — for insulting behaviour, kicked the chair from under him and fled in the midst of the clamour now reaching its peak.

Chapter Seventeen
Hamilton and the Schönfelds

The newspapers appeared with white spaces, steadily growing white spaces, as the war wore on. The censorship imposed on the press came into action when the first copies printed were shown to the censors, who then made their cuts. First a few sporadic lines, next parts of columns, then columns, and, finally, whole pages were omitted. At times there were pages retaining only a few lines which contrived to be both suggestive and frightening, doing more harm than uncensored publication of the articles omitted or mangled could have done. An odd line such as " . . . Lemberg is still in our hands . . . , " preceded and followed by blank space, created rumours and despondency — the more so if, on the following day, a place miles nearer than Lemberg was named as one where our "heroic army" was trying to stem the onslaught of the enemy, while there was no mention of the loss of Lemberg. The articles from the front, termed "the Hoefer reports", were viewed with increasing cynicism.

On a dismal day when the Hoefer reports with the insinuating cuts prepared readers for the loss of an important strategic point, Hamilton stepped out of the local bank, where he had effected the change in certain investments in keeping with both information and his ideas about the course of the war. He saw Blanca walking towards the post office. His eyes followed the briskly moving, lithe figure. He lengthened his stride and caught up with her.

They walked together past the post office. She answered his queries in friendly fashion. Yet, as before when he had seen only her back, he discerned that something was wrong. It was a feeling he could not define, because she acted and talked as on the few occasions of their previous chance meetings, and her gait was as brisk and graceful as ever.

They spoke of the scanty tidings from Willy and of his possible promotion. By now, Hamilton was sure. He stopped and, when she turned and looked up at him, he said, "You are in trouble, Blanca. Tell me. You know I want to help."

It was painful to hear words which might have been Willy's uttered in the same way he would have spoken them. She lowered her head.

He needed no further confirmation as to the nature of the trouble,

"Willy will be back shortly and we will have the wedding. Meanwhile, you had better come to live in my house."

Hamilton did not know whether she had grasped his words, as her face showed no emotion. He added, "I'll come over to see you and have a word with your father. Now, run along." He put a reassuring hand on the girl's shoulder. "And don't worry."

The next morning, he drove his gig to the Schönfeld home, and the old man received him with exquisite courtesy. Though Blanca had not spoken of Hamilton's impending visit, her father showed no emotion beyond a reserved joy.

Mr Schönfeld, as a rule equally distant in relations with his family and outsiders, shed the austere husk when, on occasions, he and Hamilton met and exchanged a few words. He had felt a warmth towards him ever since the festival day, some thirty years ago, when one of his young sons (now on the threshold of middle life) had seen Hamilton passing on horseback and asked him to come in and light the fire — Judaism proscribes manual work on the days of major festivals.

Hamilton had dismounted, tied the reins to a gatepost, entered and lit the fire and, when finished, had waved a friendly hand at the awestruck family and left.

As soon as they sat down, Hamilton began to speak. "I came here to ask you to consent to the marriage of Blanca and my son." After a moment's silence, he went on, "You might have other plans for your daughter but, as things stand, you might just as well abandon them."

Mr Schönfeld felt the force of compelling words. Before he could come to a decision, Hamilton spoke again, choosing his words, to spare the old man's feelings. "They met a lot, no doubt without your knowledge. I trust you will not live up to the custom of turning her out. I invite Blanca to live at my house."

Mr Schönfeld signalled to Hamilton to stay, got up and went to fetch both his daughter and wife. When they arrived, he was sufficiently composed to tell them of Mr Hamilton's intentions.

"You may go to live with Mr Hamilton, or you can stay here till the wedding, Blanca." He added, his reserve hardly veiling his emotion, "I consider a great honour the marriage proposal, as well as the invitation extended to Blanca."

Blanca looked at Hamilton and spoke. "Thank you, Sir. I'll stay here, for the time being anyway."

Hamilton rose and was already on the threshold when he turned and addressed the mother smilingly. "Till now, we were on terms of mere nodding acquaintance. Perhaps we'll make up for it."

Chapter Eighteen
"The Russian advance was so swift . . . "

> There won't be a sign
> on my lost grave as big as
> a man's palm . . .

The song made its debut on the cabaret stage in Budapest (as others had done, in the capital's already dimming night-life). It first appeared not as a fledgeling, with tentative wings, but as a fully-fledged bird which at once took to the air. It alighted on every lip. The soldiers sang it. So did those they left behind. The supreme command decided that it caused despondency and forbade the troops to sing it. But the ban failed. The song which voiced the men's sadness and despair as they pictured themselves dead and deserted in the vast Russian landscape, like comrades they had buried, evoked a response which no decree could quell. The response lived on, in the form of a catchy tune.

Mid-December brought a letter from Willy. He was all right, but for the shot-wound received in his thigh on the 5th. He was laid up in hospital, but he would soon be out and about and would return home.

"Blanca lovey, I shall make — nay, we shall make — the most of my leave. Ranoné's letters bring tidings of the convalescent home into which Dad has turned our house. I do not believe that much change was needed. It was always the house for both idle rich and idle poor. Even the inmates might be the same, but for the uniform — instead of Savile Row or loincloth — in which they lounge about.

"Cheer up, darling . . . . "

Blanca read the letter over and over again. The first feelings of relief gave way to doubts, then to despondency. Her movements were slow and mechanical as she put on her shawl in the kitchen, under the troubled eyes of her mother. The latter's query, as to Willy's well-being, she affirmed with a nod. Then she added, in a small voice, "He was shot in the thigh but is well enough and will be back shortly."

Already dressed to go out, she remembered her chores. She began to collect used cutlery from the breakfast-table lit by the merry winter sun. She saw the field hospital near a township and, in her mind's eye, beheld an emaciated Willy — a vision she could not account for. She feared, more than ever, that the letter was only a first glimpse of something worse to come.

Mrs Schönfeld told her to leave the washing-up and go for a walk. She bent her head as she left, looking round from the doorway as though to take in the scene — the homely and clean whitewashed kitchen, with cooking utensils and implements mirroring the bright winter morning.

With quick steps — perhaps irresolute, to the expert eye — she walked to Hamilton Manor, went through the ever open main entrance and requested a passing maid to take her to Mr Hamilton.

A playful glint in the maid's eye revealed her thought. She took Blanca to the rear entrance of the hall and motioned towards the stables, some hundred yards away.

She found him probing into the mouth of the tawny hack which his son Eddy held ready to hitch to the gig.

She was a few steps away when they noticed her. The old man stretched out both hands and she quickened her steps at the gesture. Stables, paddock, distant hills and red-roofed cottages which dotted the countryside seemed to breathe in the fresh winter morning.

After the youngster had hitched the horse, he took an awkward step towards Blanca and spoke. The words belied his movements. "I never had the pleasure to speak to you. And, now, I feel Dad wants me to go double-quick, as he wanted to see you." He gestured towards gig and horse. "May be seeing you later. Bye."

Blanca echoed the farewell and nodded in response to Hamilton's invitation to share his morning ride. He read Willy's letter as the horse took its course along the lake, which shimmered in the sun, and along the poplar-lined road between stubbled fields and scattered green patches in vast brown soil fading into the blue distance.

They overtook a wounded soldier, with one arm in a sling, who greeted them and eagerly accepted the offer to take him to his village a few miles away. Not yet nineteen, he was wounded last November in the battles around Lemberg. His open face, warm brown eyes and broad short frame disclosed that he was a Hungarian peasant, even before he spoke.

He told Hamilton, whom he knew by sight, of Willy — "the Mr Lieutenant" who was always first where help was needed, the last in retreat who brought the wounded man back to the trenches from no man's land, and the first to fraternise, "on patrol," with the Russian patrol instead of shooting it out. From the simple and halting words it emerged that "the Mr Lieutenant," though younger than most of his men, was their idol, father and friend rolled into one, who eased their burdens and even wrote their letters.

The hamlet the youngster was heading for slowly emerged, leaning against a hill. The radiance of the little white-walled cottages sent out a call to stay within the hospitable walls and forget the bruit of a crazy world.

The youth begged leave to alight and set out on the bumpy road towards his fairy world.

As they turned homeward Hamilton cleared his voice then, with some difficulty, he began.

"I know all about it — in fact, I have known for days and only in the night I decided to call on you. But I know more. The Russian advance was so swift that the hospital could not be evacuated and, with the bigger part of the battalion, fell into their hands. And it might be all for the best. Willy's out of it and cannot endanger his life with silly pranks such as we just heard about. He is in good hands. The Russian is a gallant antagonist. I know of instances where prisoners of war were received warmly — in some towns, amidst banter and showered with flowers.''

After Hamilton's words, the poplars and the shimmering lake seemed the same yet not the same, to Blanca. Still, the words had blunted her worst fears.

At nearly one o'clock they drove into the paddock, where an old groom took charge of the horse and gig. They walked into the house as a muffled gong announced it was mealtime. It shook the house into activity.

Doors opened and closed with bangs. Men in uniform, some bandaged, others limping, and white-clad women — some of them nurses — came from all directions and converged on the big dining-hall. In reading-rooms and study, huge armchairs gave forth their cargo. Billiard-rooms emptied and the last stragglers sat down while the soup was being served.

No class or rank distinction was maintained. Major sat next to private, as in olden times. This occasioned the displeasure of some but, as in olden times when no protest could dislodge the greyhounds, complaints fell on deaf ears. (Incidentally, the greyhounds had gone.)

They came upon Ranoné in her own quarters, entertaining her close friends Colonel Count Vicky Wasmer and the Colonel Padre who attended to her spiritual needs. The padre spent his frequent leaves with the Hamiltons.

Ranoné was rummaging in a drawer, when Hamilton ushered in Blanca. Though they had never spoken before, the introductory phrase fell flat in the ensuing wrangle without words. Ranoné proffered her hand, her eyes steely. In her middle thirties, she was just reaching the height of her beauty. A greenish shade under her chin suggested a measure of weariness — "the way of all flesh," went a line in her grandmother's song about the Glossy, the mill and the miller's wife. Her lips, too, might have been those of the miller's wife, "Fresh and insatiable as death.''

As they shook hands, Hamilton smiled reminiscently, then he voiced his thoughts. "Some years ago, I saw an American cartoon. Two rival beauties meet and, as they shake hands, each left hand hides a huge axe in the folds of a skirt. The ease with which they held the heavy axes called for a masterly effort only on the part of the artist. I realise, now, that the axes were symbolic. I might have brought the matter up later, but for the duel we just witnessed. I want you women to sink your differences before they are born, because I request you, Ranoné, to invite Blanca to help us.''

Ranoné answered with a pleasant "Charmed" and a few words to the girl which bore no trace of the malice she had displayed before.

Half-way through the second course, the atmosphere began to warm up. In this, no small part was played by the padre and Count Vicky.

Vicky retained a lot of his former self. When — as a lieutenant — he had pursued her with all the avidity of an ardent youth, Brydie had disarmed his ardour gently. The Russians proved less gentle. It was now the second time that he was spending months with the Hamiltons, after long stays in hospitals. He remained true to the type of the professional soldier whose battle methods had changed but little since the Crusades (in which, incidentally, more than one of his forebears had taken part). As a true cavalryman, he charged. It was devastating and would have done credit to Attila, but it was ineffectual against the Russian barbed wire defences. Russian machine-gun-fire mowed men down in thousands. Vicky himself was riddled with bullets, lesser wounds killed many a good man.

His attitude — carefree, impulsive and with no thought preceding the amusing words — impressed Ranoné. She did not fail to notice that his wit, charm and easy-flowing words were directed at Blanca as well as at her.

Blanca left her black coffee untouched. 'What next?' she thought when Ranoné took her arm, to lead her through doorways, corridors and rooms. On the way they met men recuperating after being restored by clinical means, some of whom greeted them while others just smiled.

'I would have loved her, if she had begun this way,' thought Blanca. 'Now, I know what I am up against. I hate her, the old slut, but she's lovely — like a prowling cat, a tiger. I don't hate her — I am scared. I must be on my guard.'

They met and stopped the old doctor Breuer, on his way home. He came daily to do, or supervise, some elaborate bandaging, administer an injection or just to go his round of ''Faith-healing'' in which he excelled. He read both character and malady, spoke inspired words — stories and reminiscences — which raised the spirits and supplied physics as well as advice to heal or alleviate the ailment.

They met him when he was licking from his fingers morsels of the poppy-seed cake which he had pinched from a passing tray.

Ranoné told him that Blanca was joining the crew at the right moment, so many friends had left them that they were anxiously counting the heads.

Blanca stood by absent-mindedly. She did not allow herself to be dragged from musing and only later did she remember a phrase of the doctor's about ''the hungry Hamiltons''. The words might have escaped her altogether — through her preoccupation with her thoughts — but for Ranoné's husky laugh as she repeated the phrase after they and the doctor had parted. Blanca sensed in the laughter malice bearing on her sudden arrival at the Hamiltons'.

Dining-rooms, bedrooms, corridors hardly registered. She asked a few innocuous questions about her duties, which were mere words to hide behind. Ranoné answered in the same vein, "You don't have to carve out your work. I do some of the clerical, but hate it. It's up to you, if you want to do that or chores more on the distaff side."

As Ranoné finished speaking Andrew, her oldest son, entered. "Two feet first," she termed the entry, her eyebrows raised.

"Dad sent me to look after Cinderella because, he said, you've already begun to impersonate the wicked step-ma."

Andrew's breathless words were overheard by his brother Eddy who came in, quietly followed by Itzig. "I like the wicked step-ma," Eddy said, "much more than that go-getter Cinderella. But Blanca isn't that. She is our Penelope and I appoint myself her number one suitor. That, of course, introduces a new note into the Odyssey. His brother as the principal suitor raises the plot into the highest Greek tragedy class. But here is Itzig, another suitor, not less dangerous in his dumbness. He never says a word, which makes people believe he is clever. The tone of the tragedy requires another word — perhaps taciturn."

Itzig stood there, grinning as if embarrassed. He shuffled his feet as he felt something amiss. Nor did he have any part in the sequence of the argument about the Cinderella tale's vulgarity, pro and con between the brothers, a duel of wit and violence.

Blanca knew that the boys were with her. The scene reminded her of the dream Willy had related to her; himself as two cats interlocked in a fratricidal battle.

Ranoné was not at ease at her sons' performance, their keen observation and outspokenness. She felt as though she was being stabbed, again and again. This did not improve her humour. While the battle still raged, she left — with an aside about "The Hungry Hamiltons".

BOOK III

Chapter Nineteen — **At the Vernal Equinox**

"We may, but imagination fails and the spirit shrinks before the immensity."

A dog barked in the distance, inviting a few nearer howls and barks, and again there was silence.

A side glance at Blanca, then Itzig knew that he must keep it up.

"Have you ever thought of the speed of light, which can travel the length of the equator in a split second? Yet, at times, ages go by before it reaches us from a planet of another galaxy. The other day it was calculated that a flash in the telescope was a beam of light from the Andromeda which had set forth on its journey in the Middle Ages, perhaps a hundred years before they signed the Treaty of Westphalia."

He thought that he held her. "We dwell on a puny satellite of a second-rate sun. In the vastness, in time and in space, humanity — even the greatest of us — is less than a speck of dust. Don't think I'm preaching when I say if only we could step outside — beside — ourselves, our apprehensions and sorrows, great as they might seem, could be put in their place. Otherwise, they loom large in the foreground and block our vision."

The boy's last words, quoting the old man (which he dubbed a flippant departure), warmed her more than the foregoing ones. However, philosophy can explain away anything but toothache.

She perceived the kindness of the scholar who holds nothing holy or final, the breath and breadth of the Hamilton world.

In the morning she had risen at seven, later than usual, checked the work of the nurses, spoken to the convalescents and granted their requests with a distant smile.

The heaviness she felt came in spasms. The last one was the longest. Only Itzig's presence dispelled it for a while. She knew that it was to stay all day.

She walked but in a haze, her movements and actions mechanical. She lay down at mid-afternoon and when she woke Count Vicky sat by the sofa.

The french windows led to a terrace with iron fretwork, one of the inventor's whims. The windows opened on the Vertes mountains, vanguard of the Carpathians. The mountain-tops were ablaze in the light of the setting sun against the advancing shadows of dusk. The oval mirror of the fragile rococo dressing-table embraced a sun-caressed crest and the light overflowed the frame onto the softly patterned wallpaper behind. The faint and unreal light showed up a few faded photographs and a spidery drawing of Willy, as a boy of fifteen, made by Oscar. Ranoné had given her the drawing, in a moment of fitful generosity.

Blanca's first gaze fell on Count Vicky. It gave her no pleasure. She closed her eyes. For a few minutes no one spoke, then the Count broke the silence.

"Don't pretend to be asleep. You only want me to go. You're treading ruthlessly on my feelings."

His approach had changed but little since his youth. It remained the same dated frontal attack (which, in another setting, stumbled on the barbed wire of the Russians). Yet, his histrionics became subtler and his promises vaguer, when he pleaded.

"Shall I go?" he pressed on.

"Stay if you like," said Blanca. "I'm only a bit weary."

"Of course. The clammy, sultry, air of the house, the worry about the boy, inconstant as boys are . . . . I ought not to tell you more, but I can't contain myself. Throw up everything and come with me. At my side in Vienna, sweet nostalgic city, the fountain of life . . . . "

She felt numb, but often when one of our senses fails another takes over, perhaps to compensate. Suddenly, she could see it all clearly. The promises of men when passion grips them, when they are heated or craving for affection. They even mean what they say at the moment. Some keep their words and remain unhappy ever afterwards. Some become lyrical, others inarticulate.

Aloud, she only said, "You've passed the threshold of middle age and are scared lest life slips through your fingers."

Her words touched a sore spot. Words which already filled him to bursting remained unsaid. He stood up, bowed slightly and went like one who is striving to sort out his thoughts.

He came again, on the following afternoon. He did not say so, but the sunken eyes and the hand trembling when he lit a cigarette revealed that in the night he had sought solace with the gypsies.

His remarks were cut short by a knock on the door and the solemn entry of the Colonel Padre, who stood for a moment, holding the handle of the heavy oak door, then came forward. Measured steps carried the huge bulk of his body to the bed. The rhythm remained while he pulled a chair to the bedside and sat down heavily. Only now did he ask, "How are you, child?"

The resonance of his voice, though compelling, drew no answer. Nor did her deepset eyes speak of any pleasure his visit gave her.

Count Vicky reminded her of the mole which blindly follows urges, unaware of the harm done to the crop. The padre was more than that. He had a reputation for dealing with both malingerers and women. Stories of how he had brought them to heel travelled ahead of him.

She identified him with more than one of the characters in the Viennese dramatist Schnitzler's *Reigen* (also dubbed *La Ronde*). As his features faded into the shadows she imagined, in his face, the fangs of the beast life the book portrays.

In proportion to the attentions increasingly paid her since Ranoné's departure, the usually veiled recesses in which affection dwells — and to which curiosity is a skeleton key and sexual drive the fulcrum — lay wide open with her. On his last visit, he had taken her hand and warmed it in his dry almost feminine hand — his tapering fingers could have served as models to a Florentine portrait painter. "Now," he said, "I want to put you on the road to God."

All her wisdom forgotten, she could no longer judge his stagey words. Her glowing eyes and moist lips held a promise, were the tools of sin of Christian mythology. She hung on his words which, had they been written down, would have seemed merely a mystic jumble. Yet, conveyed at that moment — a well-timed one — they conjured up a mirage of harmony in which she wallowed. Her fingers held his like tendrils. He felt her emotion falling in with his own.

That night, to her relief, a telegram summoned the Colonel Padre to the northern front, via headquarters at Shanistor.

As her time drew nearer Blanca longed, more than ever, for Willy's return. Their child was born on the night of the vernal equinox, when a gale rooted up saplings and brought down chimneys, and the moon appeared as though placed in a court: a sequence of signs which meant a dreaded omen to the villagers.

Chapter Twenty
Word came through the Red Cross

Crane bird travelling south, fly
o'er a little orphan house.
Taking sighs of my heart, knock at
the window of my house:
They won't wait in vain who expect
our return, crane bird, crane bird.

The song voiced the thoughts of prisoners who languished in the camps in far away Siberia.

The giant Russian bear had threatened to wipe out the armies of the Central Powers. More than half drowned in the Mazurian swamps its troops carried on and picked up again, in spite of being ill-equipped, ill-fed, ill-clad and badly officered by Count Vicky's Russian equivalent. Whole regiments went barefoot into battle, charging with clubs instead of bayonets. Therefore, the giant bear was forced back into its lair by way of Brest-Litovsk.

Word came through the Red Cross that Willy was well, no longer an inmate of a prison camp but on parole. Blanca clutched the letter from Hamilton, now in Vienna. The old man could also tell that Willy, though virtually free was yearning to come back.

Then the Russians surrendered and signed the humiliating Treaty of Brest-Litovsk. He (Trotsky) wore his army topcoat as romantic revolutionaries wore their capes. He smiled faintly and spoke a few words about exigency to the poet who was his close friend and added, prophetically, that the day was not far when they would be back for keeps. The poet wrote down the scene in vivid words. The verses were but short-lived. They were soon omitted, from later editions, in the new Russia.

The genius of the spiky German war-lord Ludendorff, triumphed. He had planned the Mazurian campaign to which Hindenburg gave his name. He also sent Lenin in a sealed train to Russia to soften the ground which, as he had planned, led to Brest-Litovsk.

At the same time, and with renewed vigour, he planned the blow with which to bring down the Allied Powers. The very names of the generals, von Falkenhayn, von Machensen (who wore the emblem of the Totenkopf hussars), and even the supreme head of the armed forces, von Hindenburg, conjured up the Germanic myth — the past glories, Valhalla — and the seeds of a new myth of victorious German arms were sown.

It came about otherwise. The German poet put it aptly. If we won the war, we would sleep with our hands on trouser seams, women would throw a child yearly and God himself would be a German general.

In the last desperate bid for cannon-fodder, the army doctors found fit all but stretcher cases, runs a contemporary sally. In the all-out effort the army's clergy, too, did its share. Thus, our friend the Colonel Padre was called upon. He dedicated himself to the task. His rousing speeches brought out the last remnant of a martial spirit and echoed the enthusiasm of the early days of the war, by now long extinct.

The offensive began in the west. Then it was all over, so quickly that it took the breath away. The British tanks sealed the fate of the Central Powers. The delegates signed the armistice in a railway carriage in Compiègne Forest. The aftermath embodied a sense of relief.

When the latter wore off, and they began to look round for a scapegoat, and none of the scapegoats filled the void in the public imagination, resentment sprang up.

Word went round that the war was not lost in the field, but through the politicians' stab in the back. The red prince of Baden and his cronies shoved the Kaiser off to Holland, effected the downing of arms and offered peace at any price. The Allied armies, just as exhausted as their opponents, were the most astonished at the spectacle (according to the rumour born in Germany).

Even before Brest-Litovsk there were individual cases, gradually growing into a trickle, of war prisoners who tricked and bribed their way out of Russia. The drift strengthened, after the treaty. These men did not escape the influence of the Russian upheaval; they swelled the discontent which ultimately inundated Middle Europe. They assumed power, which marked the beginning of the ill-fated ninety-nine days of the Hungarian Soviet.

Les hordes de la dernière heure — the opponents of the règime (the heroes of tomorrow) lay low or burrowed — often, held office under the communist regime.

At Budapest East Railway Station, the melancholic bustle of the war gave way to scenes such as one might have witnessed at an out of the way halt along the Baikal Lake, where Kalmuks or Ostraks arrived days ahead of the scheduled train (which might be days late). Slow-moving men, women with babies strapped to their backs, children playing amongst bedding and baskets, villagers — many still wearing the infantry tunic or boots, others in shabby black broadcloth or traditional calf's-muzzle shirts, the women in layers of pleated skirts, children barefoot regardless of the chill of early spring — all overflowed the platforms under the glass vaulting. The sun but sluggishly entered the grimy panes, alighting on faded announcements under the lofty roof. Maintenance was its lowest in the history of the Hungarian State Railways. The little repaired during the transition period was smashed up again in the Comintern Revolution and the counter-revolution which followed in turn stripped bare carriages and waiting-rooms.

At long intervals, a train backed into the hall. Before it could slow down, the scramble started. The doors were rushed at, and the windows too, in the scramble for seats. The train was full before it had come to a halt. The throng in the corridors was so dense that one could not move. The least lucky ones crowded onto the steps leading to the doors, at both ends of each carriage. Then someone said that six carriages were being added to the train. The steps suddenly abandoned, the fray started afresh.

Only a young man stayed behind, on the steps of one such train. When he realised that he could stick to his precarious seat, he stepped down to stretch his limbs. The crowd on the platform thinned out, until newcomers swelled it again.

He wore immaculate breeches and polished riding boots, and the white of an embroidered Russian shirt showed above the fur collar of his short overcoat.

A woman in her middle years, whose tight Hungarian blouse hugged firm ample breasts, beckoned from an all but glassless window and pointed at the seat beside her, a space of hardly more than a few square inches under a heap of skilfully arranged clothes. A wink of her humorous eye made him understand that he was to act like a friend if they wanted to avoid the wrath of men who, after years of adversity, came in search of seats — or food or anything to be had — with the grimness of hungry wolves.

A gust of wind ruffled his fair hair, as the young man's slaty eyes sought the nearest steps.

"Forget the corridor," the woman said. "Nip in here." She pointed at the window.

While he climbed in, with the ease of an athlete, she cleared the tiny space for herself, leaving the seat by the window for him.

He had cut his hand slightly, on a piece of jagged glass, during the manoeuvre. She blamed herself, tore a handkerchief and wrapped it round his hand.

The maternal activity gave her scope to pour out her heart against this new world where everything was crazy. She touched on the things which were uppermost in people's minds. One would have felt the validity, even without the nods and grunts of assent from other passengers.

The war which they had relished at the outset, its aftermath, the lords who hung on grimly to everything then lost all and, worst of all, "the new set-up" that requisitioned everything, took everything hidden from former plunderers.

Her words started off variations on the theme, as the train left the station and glided at walking pace along the route which the young man knew well from old-time journeys. While he listened to the evidence with which his fellow travellers bolstered their arguments, his eyes roamed over the familiar landscape.

The football ground where he had seen Aston Villa beat the combined eleven of MTK and 'Franzstadt', both leading Hungarian teams. The superiority and precision of the visitors' teamwork had suggested a world about which he had both heard and read, a more purposeful and organised world than his native Hungary: A world of green pastures and redbrick houses over which hung a mist, a world which was the world of his forebears.

Only now, while the train passed the back of the grandstand, did he translate the feelings of yester-year into words.

A man who had lost his arm on the Itonzo River related his trouble in the slow reflective manner of the peasant, smothering his spit with his heel, knocking his pipe out on the floor, filling and lighting it laboriously with one hand. His plight fitted the latest song. The buxom woman began to sing it in a soft contralto. It was the song of the handsome gypsy Kitmas who had played in a glittering café, had been called-up, "saw the realm of the Tzar and listened to the lovely Italiana's seductive song." He returned to the "right side of his heart," to his violin, but during the escape he lost an arm.

Others joined in, till the train came to a halt at 'Franzstadt' suburb. A few people pressed themselves into the already packed corridors and others clustered at the handrails, standing on the steps.

A bottle of sandy wine found its way from an old man's haversack. On its round it first reached the woman, who wiped it before she passed it on to her neighbour — as "a gesture of courtesy towards a gentleman . . . Alas, they're all heading south, like wild geese in the autumn."

The din of the steely bangs, on the railway bridge across the Danube, drowned the words. The boy's eyes followed the southbound river as it merged into the vast Hungarian plain.

Trouble, when it came, would come from the south. The reactionary forces gathered there, backed by the army of Marshal Franchot d'Espay, beyond the border on the northern fringe of the Balkan suburban settlements.

Industrial buildings, on a downward slope, glided before his eyes. The perfume factory built like a mosque with a minaret bearing — in man-sized letters — the name of the product: SAVOY. The metallic letters reflected the noonday sun. He remembered his father's comment when, as a child, he had pointed out the discrepancy between the oriental architecture and the English name of the product, "You may yet see Joan of Arc on the flying trapeze. Nay," he had corrected himself, "Anti-gone on the flying trapeze."

The words as well as the former associations came back and mingled with the slow-spoken words of the old man facing him. His shrunken pension altogether discontinued, he had come to the capital to follow up applications which had remained unanswered. He had joined the queue to see an official. At last, on the third day, he reached an underling who, after a few explanatory words from the old man, dismissed him without looking at the proffered papers. "No drones are needed in our Socialist State."

The last words roused the young man from his near reverie. Quietly, and for the first time, he spoke at some length. "I should like to take your name and address, Dad. I've got friends amongst what you choose to call 'the new mob'. They served with me, or I met them as a prisoner in Russia. Perhaps it will be of some help."

In the ensuing pause, he gathered that the old man thought that one could not be careful enough in a cock-eyed world. He added, "Or, even better, I'll give you my address and you can write if other means fail."

He jotted down: *William Hamilton, Jnr.,*
Tata,
County Komárom.

Chapter Twenty-one
"Mr Lieutenant"

Suddenly, Willy found himself the centre of an interest which they had not shown before. The natural good manners of the untutored peasants had imposed a reserve which began to wane when he showed concern for the old man's fate.

The woman turned a full face towards him and spoke, "Be a bit less cagey, young gentleman. We'd like to hear of your exploits in those far-off lands."

He felt that, again, she voiced the sentiments of the others. The sun shone into the compartment, warming them and lighting up lined expectant faces.

Embroidered haversacks and baskets were brought down, as if by silent agreement and almost simultaneously, to reveal meat, butter and white bread — in place of the customary maize bread, staple food of the town-dweller for years now — a denial in kind of the claim that everything was being taken from them by requisitioning.

Willy had neither food nor luggage with him. They plied him with food and wine.

At the great bend at Hegyeshalom, the westering sun once more inundated them. He told a few episodes. At the outset of the revolution, he was travelling to Kiev when he ran into a marauding group of Hungarians. They asked him the whereabouts of officers, whom they wanted to teach a few things now that they were freed from the scourge. They boasted that they had just hanged an artillery major of the Budapest Regiment.

Willy was assuring them that he had seen no officers when the old school fellow detailed to him as batman called out from the neighbouring carriage, "Mr Lieutenant".

"You're a lieutenant, eh?" said their leader, gleefully.

"The odds were against me," the young man told his listeners. "I could never make Janos drop formalities in public. He said they made him feel important and, besides, helped him in his not always above board dealings.

" 'No,' I answered, 'my name is Lieutenant.'

"By now Janos had joined us. The leader, pointing at me, shouted:

110

'This man says that his name is Lieutenant.'

"The shrewd lad guessed at the trouble. He drew himself to his full height, just about five feet, and said with dignity, 'What about it? Can a gentleman not bear a decent name, these days, without being waylaid by hooligans?'

"Meanwhile, he had decided on his course. Working up a rage he bellowed and went for the man. The burly fellow brushed him off easily and laughed. Everybody else laughed, too, at the heroics of little Janos. Neither could I hide a smile.

" 'All right, Lieutenant,' said the leader, 'you can't be the worst bastard when your man stands up for you like that. You can go. Peace be with you.' And they left."

The October revolution at St. Petersburg, the sailors' rising, the fervent idealism of the workers, their belief that they were forging ahead to a better world, came to life in Willy's even words. The latter swayed his fellow travellers, stolid peasants who dreaded the dictators of the proletariat.

"It was different here," said the woman. "Look what happened to our parson. The 'Lenin boys' came to our village from Budapest in two heavy lorries. They fetched the parson from the vicarage, stood him on a stool in front of the church, with the noose round his neck. His wife arrived on the scene screaming as though out of her mind. The terrorists, armed with revolvers and hand-grenades, stood around holding the unarmed villagers at bay and met dark looks and curses with laughs.

"The wife threw herself on her knees in front of the brute who was leader. He said that if she kicked the stool from under her husband's feet his life would be saved. She did as she was told and our good parson died."

"There is nothing which could excuse murder and, worst of all, in a revolution it is often the innocent who suffers," reflected Willy. "Vengeance is paying off the old scores raked up by the worst elements who are out to loot or to give vent to the cruel streak which is part of most men's make-up. They derive pleasure from inflicting pain like some children, which makes it worse, and they are both methodical and calculating. The Revolution brings the best as well as the worst to the fore.

"The same Hungarian gang which hanged officers also hanged Czechs. The age-old hatred which had, amongst others, a religious origin (long since forgotten while the hatred stayed) was fostered down the centuries by the Habsburg rulers for their own end. The killers' instinct found justification and assumed the force of religious fervour. The Czechs did the same. They hanged the Hungarians. Then their bands united into a great force which fought the Russian Revolution and which monopolised the Trans-Siberian railway and left Russia for Japan with all the treasures and things they could move. Killing runs amok. They found a name for such exploits in Greek history: Anabasis. The great saga made respectable what was but a riot of burning, pillage and rape.''

At the back of his mind, Willy heard his comrades at the seminary of St. Petersburg taunt him as a bourgeois intellectual who interprets things according to his liberal upbringing instead of in the Marxist sense — or to what its apologists call Marxism. "Of course, the intellectual cannot easily be regimented but he is, and always was, the true revolutionary,'' he mused.

"Washington, Lafayette, Kropotkin, Lenin, Trotsky, Marx came from the working class. All determined men, some fiery, others quiet, others again glowing with an icy passion. Yet, the intellectual who has kept alive the spark, has prepared and carried the revolution is discredited. The man with brawn, the blacksmith, the foundryman, is at sea when he comes to power; he turns into 'Jack in office'. Frightened, he resorts to cruelty. Only by killing — 'liquidating' is the word — the opponent can he hope to find peace. 'The greatest good for the greatest possible number'; but the sense of guilt is a very strong urge in us and he can find no peace of mind. The man whose hands are calloused is paragon of the age.''

The woman touched his sleeve gently, "You're not with us, Mr William,'' she said.

"I only wanted to find a better answer than my former platitudes. Here is a partial, but perhaps more telling answer. Our cobbler told me this, during the Balkan wars, when I was still a child: "The Turks caught a Komistadji — *franc-tureur* — Captain, a formidable partisan who had harassed them for a long time. They had put a price on his head and, when they caught him, tortured the man by tying him to a tree near a swamp. Soon, he was covered with mosquitoes. When no one was looking the guard, who felt sorry for him wanted to drive off the mosquitoes, but the partisan asked him not to. 'Their thirst is quenched and their sting hurts no more,' he said. 'If you drive them away, new ones will come and my pain will begin anew.'

"In our case, the tale is true, but with a diffference. When the transition is over and both irresponsible elements and greed brought under control, everybody will have the opportunity to live a good life because there is enough in the world for all of us.''

The train rolled along at a walking pace. Someone in the corridor said that caution was needed, as the line might be wrecked by the Whites. The rumour caused no stir amongst the people of the soil.

As the afternoon became more and more chilly, Willy covered the window with a horse-blanket at the old man's request. At twenty-past six they stopped at Bicske, the little market town half-way to Willy's home town. Soon, it became known that they would stop here for the night. Willy decided to walk the rest of the way. The others felt sorry at his departure. He knew that they had taken to him.

They shook his hand and he patted the woman on the cheek in place of thanks for her parting words of warning that, in these odd times, he had better look out for footpads.

The peaceful countryside belied her words. The brown fields reminded him, unaccountably, of the Thirty Years War. 'No ominous sign, no sign whatsoever, that perhaps a few miles away upheavals are taking place, men being killed in the name of an abstraction — the hammer and sickle now, king and country before, and still earlier the cross — but deep down for reasons we cannot fathom. Did father have a glimpse that this was Nature's way to restrain man from overrunning the earth? Or the bison, killed off senselessly and now nearly extinct? Or the flying ants? Or the Scandinavian rat — what is its name — which walks into the sea, in droves, to destruction? Shall we ever know why? She sends the plagues, phylloxera and the foot and mouth . . . . We beat one. Then she thinks up another. Can we ever cheat Nature? *Naturam expellas furca, tamen . . . .* '

Above him, in the hillside and about a quarter of a mile to the right, gaped the cavern 'The Hole of Selim'. His thoughts took a new turn. 'Will people always have to seek refuge? Will it always be hunters and hunted? I don't know what happened here, beyond the fact that they hid from the Turks. Did they fall into their hands? Were they harmed by the sulphurous fumes? The intelligence never touched me. Do we feel for the sufferer only when we are witnesses of the plight? Some cherish the sight of suffering, they wallow in it. Why does that make me see red? I half killed the corporal when he baited that slow-witted peasant. Nature again. It is her special method for my kind and hastens my doom.'

His measured strides took him past farmsteads and gardens, across open fields, while he followed the sun, and after sundown, when trees and hills appeared as silhouettes against the western sky. He saw them as in a mirror; they did not reach the machinery of his thoughts, but were signs along a known route.

He groped his way in the darkness, after midnight, through the unlit streets and narrow passages of his home town. At last, he turned into the wide main street and passed the hotel, which looked deserted but for a single muted light behind the portico. Next door, just across a side-street, sprawled the Town Hall, grim and ramshackle. Willy felt its chill, the hostile indifference and inequity which he associated with ruling; the harsh treatment of the poor, the bakshish, remains of the bygone Turkish world. Or does it go further back? To the time or even beyond the time when Ranck, the Cimber, drank the blood of the Town Clerk from the skull of the Provost on the steps of the Town Hall? There were no steps now.

A figure stepped from the doorway, then folded up. Bracing himself, the man turned to the wall, thrust his forearm between forehead and wall and rested. Willy helped him while he vomited. 'Surely, they beat and tortured him?'

"I'll take you home," he volunteered.

H

"Go away," groaned the man. "It's a first-rate party."

Then, Willy smelt the drink.

"Come, sonny," said the man. "I'll take you in." With drunken obstinacy, he held on to Willy.

They went in, groped their way through the yard by the dim light of a gale lantern, passed the heavy door of the jail and landed at the open door of a verandah which belonged to the flat of the resident jailer.

Chapter Twenty-two
Red Liz

Willy remembered the burly man with bushy eyebrows and a reputation. More than once, he put a man against a wall and shot a blank cartridge at him. Such 'leg-pulls' had earned the jailer the reputation of a 'joker'.

His was the first face Willy saw, now. And his voice was the first to articulate words in the midst of the din.

"Now, now, what a surprise to see young Master H. His father and his old lady beat it while the going was good. So did Count Francis" (successor to Count Moritz Esterhazy, who had left for Tibet to become a Bhuddist monk) "and . . ."

By now, his drunken voice was the only one heard. The grog-blossom on his nose seemed to glitter with dew, through the smoke and spirit fumes.

Above the mist of heavy cigarette smoke, the ceiling appeared. Paying no heed to the ranting, Willy surveyed the scene. On Scherz the jailer's right, sat a dark, pursed lipped, man whose features suggested the oriental.

"Take that smirk off your face," the jailer bellowed and, in tones a shade lower, said to his neighbour, "This is the first time since you've taken over, Comrade Lantos, that a member of" — here he fumbled as if looking for the words.

Comrade Lantos came to the aid, "The ancient régime," while his dark eyes caressed his neighbour, who sat above him, on an office desk, her shapely leg against his upper arm.

Only once before had Willy seen "the Red Baroness", as the schoolgirl baroness, Lisbeth Wasmer was known. Their smiles met. The low neckline showed her Rubenesque endowment.

"I trust Comrade Lantos will make an example of what happens when these rats try to sneak back?" Scherz the jailer added.

"Of course," Lantos said solemnly, and patted the back of his neighbour's calf. "My secretary will take notes."

"Kill him," shrieked Red Liz.

"Drop your bourgeois phraseology, my little one," suggested Lantos. "Liquidate is the word. Shout it!"

But Liz refrained. She knew that he was mocking her.

115

Too late, it came to Willy that the sign the jailer gave boded no good. He received a hefty kick in the backside which dashed him against the jailer. In that second, as often in a crisis, he beheld the whole scene.

The half-hearted interest of the 'Lenin boys' — they were used to it. In any case, the affair was mismanaged. There was no baiting of the victim, no preliminaries to put the audience into the right mood.

In the parted moist lips, half-closed eyes and head thrown back, he saw the tensed up joy of the baroness. He also saw a futile move on the part of Lantos, as if the latter wanted to prevent the scene.

A right hook from the jailer sent him back, sprawling. He had another glimpse of the baroness, of the provocative crossed legs drawn up under her chin. He remembered the Pole who had advised passing out as soon as the beating started. For a split second he struggled as to whether to take the advice, then he passed out.

Comrade Lantos brushed away the caressing hand of Red Liz. He felt queasy, but took care to show no weakness. In a sharp low voice he said that if anything like this took place again, without his express order, there would be trouble. His words sobered the revellers and, as he left, he ordered the jailer to take ''Mr H.'' in hand and have him restored to full strength, ''sharp at noon''.

With the help of his henchmen, the jailer took Willy to his bedroom, where he dismissed them. He undid his buttons and slipped a hand into his breast pocket. The wallet housed, next to a letter from Hamilton Senior, an order from the Central Committee of the C.P. to work with, and give every assistance to, Comrade Lantos.

He reflected for a second only. From then on, he acted quickly. He fetched a bottle of chloroform, sprinkled a rag and put it on the young man's face. He read the letter with care. It was a factual account of Ranoné's illness, the reason for the journey to Vienna.

'' . . . . Her urges and inclinations made it obvious that she was ill. I may call it, pompously, psychosomatic; but every illness is psychosomatic, save for effects of the proverbial tile falling from the roof.

''I took her to Prof. Freund. Cancer of the uterus. All her pelvic organs were inflamed, which accounted for her wild love life. I don't think she will last out the year. I'm staying put. In the Wirbel Laronde home she can forget . . . ''

The jailer took the rag from the boy's face, massaged his heart and poured brandy between his teeth. Slowly, he brought him round.

He looked into his slaty blue eyes and, after a while, told him in a voice atremble with emotion how sorry — how terribly sorry — he was. The excess was due solely to his drunkenness, he said, and he would go to all lengths to make good. His tone sounded genuine enough, yet could not altogether cheat Willy's ear.

The young man wanted to give a reassuring answer but, as he turned to the jailer, he felt the pain in his lumbar region. He remained silent, but slowly began to feel sorry for the man after the latter had treated his injuries with compresses and his swollen lips with an embrocation.

The man went out, closing the door quietly behind him, and departed into the spring night. The dark whipped his fear into panic. He ran, and instinctively dodged trees, bushes and other obstacles, for, as in a magnetic field, they seemed to strive towards the same direction. The few minutes which took him to the semi-baroque mansion turned him into a drowning creature who would grasp even at a straw.

He knocked on the window-pane then, as he could endure his feelings no longer, he knocked again with his fist. Contrary to his expectation, the sound was muffled, but this soothed his panic.

The inner pane opened cautiously, then Red Liz recognised the looming figure and tore open the outer window. "What the hell . . . . "

"Liz," he said, "something terrible has happened. I must talk to you."

"Lantos won't break your neck, not yet anyway. And I never want to see you here."

"Not that, Liz. It's the end."

She stood back from the window as the bulky yet astonishingly agile man climbed in. He fell on his knees. "You must save me, only you can." He held her hand, then lower arm, and pressed the former to his mouth.

"Pull yourself together," she told him. The edge had gone from her voice.

He sank into a chair with head buried in his hands. "Liz," he said, "I must be out of my mind to remind you, now, of all I have done for you. You must help me. Young Hamilton is the other boss, or perhaps the real boss. I found a chit in his wallet."

She saw herself again as the protegée of the upstart who had unobtrusively passed her on to Lantos. The jailer's action had saved her fortune and given her power. She felt the wrath of the debtor, which only grew at the memory of the jailer's words. "You were the Red Baroness. Now you're the Red Liz. Worlds come and worlds go, only the Hungarian gentry stays."

Yet, she spoke honeyed words. "I see. I'll come at ten. I want no one around. Go. And don't worry."

Quietly, she opened the door and walked over to the bed. She looked round for a chair then, after a second's hesitation, sat down on the edge of the bed close to the young man's face.

She remembered experiments she had made with sleeping governesses, gently guiding the sleeper's hand into a bowl of warm water, and the pleasing results and how a former boy-friend had beaten her for the same trick. She laid a caressing hand on Willy's cheek. The stroking hand must have conveyed her growing restlessness. He awoke suddenly.

"Boy," she said, "I was simply broken-hearted, but it couldn't be averted. The jailer and his cronies had finished with you before we realised what was going on.''

'I can believe every word — every veiled husky word of hers — they obscure my vision of her tense face and crossed shapely legs,' he thought, but stayed silent.

Her words became hesitant. ''Your eyes are reproachful,'' she said and reached the brink of breaking into sobs. Slowly she turned her head away, to hide a tell-tale tear, but her heaving bosom gave her away.

She felt his reassuring hand on her own, which went on caressing his face. Haunted by the slaty eyes which she had noticed when she saw him once, years ago, she spoke in barely audible tones. She slid from the bed and pressed her parted lips on his swollen mouth.

Chapter Twenty-three
Comrade Lantos

Willy entered the whitewashed, sparsely furninshed, office. Lantos stood at the second window on the left, his attention held by the busy street scene:

Schoolchildren were pouring from the Franciscan monastery, to the accompaniment of the midday Angelus bells, though noon was well past. Or, did the noonday ghost only play tricks?

If he did, they were not so obvious as the tricks of the local master decorator who had painted a huge mural of St. Francis in a baroque stucco frame, a well-fed confident monk who prayed as though asking for the help of the Lord; but the master had drawn inspiration from gaudy German oleographs in the spirit of the Assissi legend . . . .

The best part of a minute had gone, before Lantos turned, "Assissi has deviated from his prototype nearly as much" — he pointed a thumb over his shoulder — "as the churches from real Christianity."

"He looks like the label on a French cognac," came Willy's quick riposte, "but perhaps it is better for him to swim with the current — his image, at any rate — otherwise, we might know him as but a heretic."

The two men looked at each other. The link was forged.

"But, what about this deviation?" bantered Willy, pointing at the replica of Michelangelo. "Though it's aesthetically perfect, and whenever I see it, I am overwhelmed by pity (for humanity). Besides, this may be the only office of authority in the world where the statue stands and where one pleads for humanity. The man put his finger on the ills of the toiling masses" — he indicated the small line drawing of Marx — "the man in whose bearded photograph I saw the mental giant just as Leonardo's self-portrait presents us with an early Italian saint. Is this deviation? — Perhaps it is not," added Willy. "I recognise Oscar's hand, so he must be back. He can draw character as Goya did. But was he not misled? The artist who made concessions to no one might have been carried by his zeal and the chance to work for his fellow men.

"When they sent me to the seminar" — he looked searchingly at Lantos — "some called it the school for agitators — I had to fight against the slant thought up by the clever boys (gifted people, trained Marxists) both the enthusiasts and the opportunists; however, most of

119

them had one thing in common; the first organised thought they had ever met was Marx and, without all that came before, they each turned into a little Omar Calif. Need I say more about deviation?''

Lantos made a slow gesture towards the chair beside Willy. They sat.

'Informer? Komissar? No,' reflected Lantos. Then, without dismissing the idea, he began haltingly, ''If you let your tongue run away half as much at the seminar, you were a marked man: bourgeois, liberal and any other man in my stead would say — again, in your lingo — *agent provocateur*. My instinct does not warn me against you. It matters little. Kronos eats his offspring, so it is of little importance when my turn comes. I need exchange and, in this desert, you're the only one I can talk to. We're still in transition, the theoretician like me can still hold a post; the new artistic movement seeped mysteriously into Russia, perhaps in the same sealed wagon in which Lenin went, but for how long? Our days are numbered. Both the mediocre doctrinaire and the opportunist will supersede us. I indulge in prophecies, but so did Marx and my words may yet come true.

''In this respect he erred, because not even genius can escape the Zeitgeist that the universe is but a huge mechanical system which man has penetrated, will survey and eventually parcel out. For him nothing counted but the mind as though, in reality, man was governed by the mind. All this detracts little from his genius but plays havoc with his prophecies — or, let me say forecasts, as it would have pleased the rationalist in him. His forecasts suffer from clear formulation, which is not the case with Nostradamus and the older oracles on whose cloudy statements one can put different constructions.

''But such views on every level play into the hands of the Messrs Scherz-Legpulls who find us an ideal scapegoat for every set-back. Imagine what they can do when their sadism is backed by righteous indignation against 'defeatists, deviationists and other rats'. Then they torture and kill with gusto. And in times of crisis they lose their heads and resort to the only means they know; murder.''

''You speak as if there were no defence against excesses,'' commented Willy. ''Even if they hinder, the wheels go round.''

''The very thing,'' said Lantos. ''The komissar who was sent in to prevent former Tsarist officers from 'running-over' — the police nark, as an institution, to an extent which never existed before — is demoralising enough; but the real trouble is that, by and large, the posts of coercion go to the worst elements — just as those people with the inclination become hangmen.''

''I agree with much of what you say and much lives in me in a flux.'' Willy now became halting, as if he had to choose his words. ''Still, socialism will come into its own. Much too great a part of the world has been conditioned — and this increases daily — for its growth to be arrested.''

''I don't doubt it,'' Lantos took him up again, ''but I'm in despair that it will follow the classical course, just like Christianity which banished a higher culture — yet did not bring the charity to man which is its unspoken claim — and in whose name so much cruelty and bloodshed were done that I shudder lest the development of socialism should take the same form.''

''Don't you think that your conscience hinders you from doing your best, Lantos? Now you rule according to accepted precepts and with that indefinable something which one needs for ruling. Yet — you know it best — you have to curb both your flagellant spirit and your inclination to see too much ahead. You might fall into the same pit as Marx as a prophet. Even if we accept the view that every great movement begins as a tragedy and ends as a farce, we cannot deny that the lot of the unprivileged has improved since the Pyramids; the line is clearly perceptible.''

Lantos smiled wanly. ''I would like you to have the last word and I hope we'll have other discussions but, just now, I would like to say a word about last night. Or, do I have to?''

''No.'' Willy shook his head.

''Very well, then. And'' — slowly — ''this is harder. Would you accept a position with us? It is not my idea, but Red Liz's, and she made it clear that you should know that it's hers.''

''I'm already with you,'' said Willy, ''and there were moments — I like histrionics — when I wanted to hand you my credentials, but not after our talk.''

''Does Liz know about this?'' Lantos studied Willy through narrowed eyes, as he indicated the document.

The young man withstood the gaze. ''I told no one.''

''I see.'' Lantos read the document again. ''Anyway, you're the informer, after all.''

''I am, but your instinct may be right; it didn't warn you.''

''Well, where do you want to work? Or, perhaps we could have twin desks; then I could still keep an eye on you, or the illusion of it.''

The door opened noiselessly, and Red Liz came in. Her charcoal-grey dress, inches longer than the current fashion, stressed a supple body. Her glance brushed, only brushed, Willy and her full lips broadened into a smile when she spoke to Lantos. ''What have I done now?''

The healthy ivory-coloured teeth, behind lower lip drooping a shade, sent a shiver down Willy's spine.

'What can I see in her? Her big hips and big bosom as they move in her own rhythm, now muted like the quiet before the tempest; the ill-defined mouth which trembles with suppressed emotion when it breaks into a smile, a mirthless smile.

'What a change from the awkward little girl of a few years ago, with pipe-stem legs and averted eyes, who was seen home from school by a purple-clad mother — the latter's skirts sweeping the dust, while her bosom nearly toppled over her corseted wasp waist, and a black cartwheel hat shaded broad features which spoke of the rich black Hungarian soil from which she sprang . . . '

Baron Sigurd — Sigi to the world — married his buxom young peasant mistress when his hungry relations had tried to impress upon him the wisdom that more careful spending would be to his own interest and to the best interest of the estate (given to the family by St. Stephen, in the steps to curb his own Hungarian nobles, nearly a thousand years ago) or, rather, the fraction of the estate left after Baron Sigi's activities at Monte Carlo, Longchamps and Ascot as well as lion-hunting in Africa and summer hunts in the Arctic.

Thinking otherwise, Baron Sigi gave his name to the then seven-month-old Liz. He died shortly afterwards. His smile, on the deathbed, might have been evoked at the thought of the contest between the tight-fisted wife and the noble clan.

In seven years, she won the case on all counts; but the greater part of the estate went to the lawyers. The little girl was nurtured on the hatred and bitterness of the struggle, as well as the bitterness at the county's refusal to accept the widow. Man gave to man her door handle; men who wanted her to exchange her own shining coat of arms for their lesser ones. Her appetite was great; her fancy varied like the wind, and the suitors usually left poorer than they had come.

Liz's eyes met Willy's. Her black-rimmed eyeballs evoked for him the image of the tiger, cold glassy callousness which can flame into senseless cruelty. Something dissolute in the big, moist mouth and practices of which he had heard mingled with the memory of the parted lips which had nearly smothered him in the morning and the song 'To close with a kiss your eye'.

Aloud he only said, "I'll send over an old escritoire of my father's which, you may agree, will fit well into the surroundings." More formally, he added, "And, from tomorrow, I am at your disposal, Comrade Lantos."

He strode beside the River Glossy. On the opposite bank was Blanca's unkempt garden. 'How little I think of her, she is so far from my thoughts!'

He stepped onto the bridge. The river shimmered in the sunshine, tadpoles basked with tails wagging or shot forward for some unknown reason. From the mill, upriver, a deep male voice sang —

"When you come to the café you'll think of me, you fair lad,
They've already found a bride for you,
They will bury me on your wedding day . . . "

The elation he had felt gave way to uneasiness. The current popular song with the Victorian theme touched something in him. He wanted to ward it off.

He began to fill in the gaps in the song. 'The young man is tall and slender, with a ready smile on his pale face, and a gold crown over his right molar. He works in a dingy office; at night he loses his money to the gypsy horse-copers, who have arrived on the eve of the fair, and to the other unsavoury clients of the cashier woman. After the card battles, she consoles the desperate "blond lad" and the day comes when she makes good the monies he has embezzled. She mothers him, which he finds increasingly tiresome; his otherwise mild language becomes foul when he is with her — *la nostalgie de la boue* — but she doesn't seem to mind. He is so utterly different from the ageing commercial traveller or the fat pork butcher. Then he marries the pretty girl, as arranged by his family.'

The absence of bustle in Willy's home was something new to him. The empty armchairs, the threadbare and faded upholstery showing the horsehair in patches. 'A bygone world,' he thought; 'dead, like Chinoiserie or regency.'

In the hall, as he turned to the steps, he noticed the dog — an old fat greyhound — his long tail motionless and incongruently thin for his large body. It was Shady Deal, the one-time champion.

"Even you, old rascal," he said gently, "feel embarrassment." He said no more, he felt a lump in his throat. The dog dragged its heavy body to him — the hind part was lamed — pressed its head against his knee and looked at him from wise old eyes.

He stroked the dog's head and scratched him behind the ears. 'If I

123

leave him, he will drag himself beside me' he reflected and, so, he carried the dog in his arms in his search through dusty and curtained rooms.

From his father's study, voices came to him. His brother Andrew and Itzig were apparently discussing a mathematical problem. As he soon realised, from their words to and fro, they were about to arrive at the formula for measuring the kinetic energy of a moving body.

Standing at the door, with Shady Deal in his arms, he spoke the formula.

The boys turned towards the door. After a second's silence, they kicked the chairs from under them, rushed at Willy and embraced him with the dog between them.

He wanted to ask about Blanca, but was cut short by remarks about his battered face. He countered them, "What about food, boys?"

They brought him bacon smothered in red paprika, maize bread (from 1917, maize had taken the place of wheat) and ersatz coffee made from baked corn. Willy ate the bacon like the peasants. He took it between his left thumb and forefinger, strengthening the hold with the middle finger; with the last two fingers of the same hand, he pressed a slice of bread to his palm. He contemplated the bacon for a while, with open pocket-knife in his right hand, before he cut off a slab. "For years, I haven't indulged in this ritual," he said.

"Yes, the food was different," he answered the youngsters' querying eyes. "And the people — or perhaps not the people, but everything was in a flux, and facets of human nature turned from one, like the far side of the moon, which one might have sensed or read about suddenly confronted one. At times, one was tossed about like a cockle-shell on the waves. The simile is wrong, really. The waves of passions of which I speak are unpredictable. But the storm passed over you, too, though I don't yet know with what intensity and like to think you were on the fringe."

"We had more than a little spasm of it," Andrew answered, "just after the boys left for Vienna, when Mother wanted to see us before the surgeons took her in hand (I suppose she knew). I stayed at home because my leg was in plaster, after a rugger match. Eddy and Guy are going on with their studies in Vienna; Father thought they might as well better their cock-eyed German.

"They arrived in Vienna just before the collapse. The fresh breeze, which had sprung up under the short-lived Karolyi Government, became a whirlwind which swept the last remnants of reaction from the face of the earth."

Itzig gave Willy a quick look, but the latter's face remained impassive.

"Once, the Lenin boys came from Budapest, in two armoured cars," Andrew went on. "They are the terrorists reputed to be above the law.

"They were swinging out in their race from Tuck Shop Corner into the Square, towards the bell tower, when they suddenly pulled up alongside me in the midst of a hellish screech of brakes and wheels.

"Out popped a handsome face. 'I say, lad, tell me the way to Amon, the ex-mayor.'

"My first reaction was to baffle him. 'Alright, lad,' he laughed, displaying two rows of lovely teeth, 'hop in.'

" 'What for?'

" 'Otherwise, you may not know where he lives — perhaps not even have heard of him. After all, one can't hear of everybody in a town of 5,000 — even if he happened to be the boss.'

" 'I'm on my way to school.'

" 'Never mind.' The smile had vanished. He pronounced the name which terrified the land. 'Just tell them that you helped Joska Czerny.'

"Thoughts raced through my mind. The nearest house was fifty yards away. I saw the muzzle of the machine-gun. Leisurely, Czerny eased himself from the seat. He was a head taller than I, about your height and even broader than you. From his peaked leather cap — through short jacket, breeches and leggings — to his boots, he wore black leather.

" 'You did your best, lad, but you can't beat it. Not because of that' — he jerked his head towards the machine-gun: 'I use it only in battle — but because I can still run a hundred metres inside seconds. Now then, I can't haggle with you half the morning.'

"He drove slowly, asking me about Amon; about the seed he was to distribute among the smallholders but used for his own ends, his witticisms, the somersaults he used to throw, his obscene crack when Aunt Julie asked him how to fertilise the tomatoes.

" 'You're shielding the wrong one,' said the man at the wheel and I felt that I was wrong when he added in a reflective manner, 'When we want to clean up the dirt.'

"After he'd learned my name, he said that Dad, too, was on his list. 'You can't mention my father and Amon in the same breath,' I said heatedly.

" 'Perhaps not,' came the prompt answer. We stopped. 'John Amon is the name,' he told his henchmen, over his shoulder, and they jumped from the car and surrounded the house. You never saw such a sinister lot, like the buccaneers in the films. A one-eyed fellow called out in a stentorian voice, 'John Amon, come out. John Amon!' Apparently, it was the routine.

"The short stocky man appeared on the threshold, his thin lips and face drained of blood. His wife ran out, passed him and threw herself at the feet of the one-eyed man, whose knees she embraced while protesting that her husband was innocent.

"Joska looked at Amon, quietly indicating with his eyes that he was to enter the second car. Then the pretty younger daughter came out, still adjusting a rebel curl, and walked up to Czerny.

"You can't have forgotten the pretty Rose," digressed Andrew. "Only recently she played up to the Styles boy, who shot himself.

" 'Spare my father,' she demanded.

" 'Why?' asked Czerny with a smile which, I think, he reserved for women. 'He is no good, is he?'

" 'He isn't, but he is my father.'

" 'As good a reason as any; but, suppose I take you instead?'

"Rose's eyes held his throughout the tense scene, then she cast them down and even blushed — By Jove, she can put up a show!

" 'Now, go to your school, you rascal,' he called to me. Making a gesture, he said for all to hear that he hadn't even known who Amon the mayor was till I warned him that he was to argue it out with the pistol and, at end of the sentence, he bashed his holster. By the time he had finished he was close to me and, under his breath, he said, 'If you ever want anything just call me or send word, lad.'

"Itzig said that Czerny's rough words were to save me from possible wrath. I became a hero overnight. Variations on the story sprang up. One of them was that I hanged Amon with my own fair hands, but this was not altogether believed because Amon carried on as before, indulging in his daily 'twenty-one' game with his cronies, at the café, on the very day his daughter ransomed him. The version that I cut the rope when he was already dangling won most adherents.

"With few exceptions, the monks lay low. Other masters, mainly the young ones, enthused about the new world and led the processions in which we shouted ourselves hoarse. 'Long live the revolution of the proletariat and other worthy causes — such as the masters, the handsome legs of a passing young woman etc., all sharks in the Indian Ocean, etc.'

"The young history master, in his zeal, even wanted to punish Itzig for rejecting office in the Students' Council of the Sixth Form. His old man had said that a Jew shouldn't meddle in politics. As soon as something goes wrong, he gets the blame.

"I should really have told you, first of all, that the times when we students could be pushed around are over. Equality and the Students' Councils see to that. Our zealous puppy had to climb down. His argument, from Roman history, that 'who is not with us is against us' found approval with the lickspits but they, too, were silenced by Shilling (who was elected in Itzig's place) — for the reason, he said, that he is one of those who are on principle against anything that comes *ex-cathedra* — and by me, as I'm the other member, on the grounds that in a free Socialist Republic a man can follow his conscience."

Willy smiled, "How would you define this brand of socialism, Itzig?"

"It isn't based strictly on doctrine," came the answer, "it is socialism of the heart which, perhaps, branches out from an older trend in socialism than the current one.

"The whole town," went on Itzig, "has been fired by the idea of democracy. Yes, *demos* the people was discovered and 'labour' people who never did a day's work and were proud of it, are saying today that work ennobles. The gym master tabled the motion to ban ancient authors who refer to *misera plebs* and *odi profanum vulgus*.

"But perhaps I should tell you the aftermath of Joska Czerny's visit — or Andrew should, because he was involved."

Full of interest, Willy turned to his brother.

"Well," began Andrew, "the sailors came over from Komárom and threatened to raze the Town Hall to the ground.

"No, let me begin with Czerny's departure. He turned over to Lantos the prisoners who were in the second car, suggesting that they were too small fry to be taken to Budapest and that he should deal with them at his discretion. Lantos in his turn thought it best to let them go home, after a day or two, when he had lectured them about the fruits of socialism and admonished them to co-operate.

"Lantos duly delivered the lecture but Scherz the jailer, contrary to orders, was still holding them after a week. Among the hostages, as they were called, was Rade's father, who had been in command of the monitors — gunboats — covering the retreat from Rumania.

"He was very popular with all ranks and when his crew heard of his detention they came over and, as one man, demanded the immediate release of the Corvette Captain Rade Macher.

"For days, Lantos had been absent. Scherz tried to temporise and, then — you should have seen the sailors! — They were reported to have been in the forefront of the rebellion; each of them looked a walking arsenal and they decided to storm the Town Hall. They even lined up the two cannons from the Napoleonic wars.

"By now both Rade and I arrived on the scene. 'Go it, boys!' shouted Rade. 'He's my dad!'

" 'Hurrah!' the sailors shouted.

" 'Come on, Andrew.' Rade dragged me. 'We'll shed our last drop of blood for the *prolétaire* freedom' — or something to that effect.

"Before I could say much, we were being carried on the shoulders of the sailors. They might have used us as battering rams, for all I know! But Scherz relented. The 'hostages' came pouring into the street, from the main entrance."

Leaving the boys — and Shady Deal — Willy resumed his quest. Lost in thought, he wandered through rooms, doorways and corridors. As he turned a corner he came face to face with Blanca, who was carrying the baby. The latter pressed to her bosom, she sighed "Willy" and fainted into the strong arms, which, in the nick of time, closed round her and the child.